HEARTBREAK

Also by Craig Raine:

The Onion, Memory
A Martian Sends a Postcard Home
Rich
History: The Home Movie
Clay. Whereabouts Unknown
A la recherche du temps perdu
Haydn and the Valve Trumpet
In Defence of T. S. Eliot
T. S. Eliot
Collected Poems, 1978–1999
'1953'

HEARTBREAK

Craig Raine

Atlantic Books
London

First published in Great Britain in 2010 in hardback by Atlantic Books,
an imprint of Grove Atlantic Ltd.

The moral right of Craig Raine to be identified as the author
of th̶

The extracts from 'Stop all the Clocks' and 'Anthem for St. Cecilia's Day',
Collected Poems, W. H. Auden (Faber and Faber, London, 2004) © The Estate
of W. H. Auden and reprinted by permission of Faber and Faber Ltd.

The extract taken from 'Little Gidding', *Complete Poems and Plays*, T. S. Eliot
(Faber and Faber, London, 2004) © The Estate of T. S. Eliot and reprinted by
permission of Faber and Faber Ltd.

'I Wish I Were In Love Again'. Words by Lorenz Hart, Music by Richard Rodgers
© 1937 (Renewed) Chappell & Co., Inc. (ASCAP)

1 3 5 7 9 10 8 6 4 2

A CIP catalogue record for this book is available from the British Library.

ISBN: 978 1 84887 510 4

Printed in Great Britain

Atlantic Books
An imprint of Grove Atlantic Ltd
Ormond House
26–27 Boswell Street
London WC1N 3JZ

www.atlantic-books.co.uk

For my son Moses,

who gave me the idea for this book and
one of its best jokes

'The man in the brown macintosh loves a lady who is dead'

– James Joyce, *Ulysses*

Contents

Stop All the Clocks

Miss Havisham has had her heart broken. She has been jilted at the altar itself. In *Great Expectations*, Dickens gives us standard-issue, instantly recognisable, consensual heartbreak but in a dramatically lit version. She is still in her trousseau, her veil a cobweb, presiding over the ruins of her wedding reception. The cake is like an opera house after an earthquake. There is a Beckettian drama of dust thick over everything. Like the three principals in *Play*, Miss Havisham is trapped in a constricted vicious circle of repetition. Because her heart is broken, nothing now works, not time itself. We enter an oubliette that remembers only one event. Dickens doesn't tell us Miss Havisham's Christian name. It could be Trauma. Or Aporia. All the clocks are stopped at twenty minutes to nine, the very moment when her heart was broken.

'Stop all the clocks', Auden's cabaret song, is about the failure of love – about heartbreak. It isn't about the death of a lover, as readers commonly assume – including Richard Curtis, the script-writer of *Four Weddings and a Funeral*. Auden's song (written for Hedli Anderson) is too hyperbolically comic to be seriously elegiac: 'Prevent the dog from barking with a juicy bone'; 'Let the traffic policemen wear black cotton gloves'; and (the source of the mistake) 'Let aeroplanes circle moaning overhead / Scribbling on the sky the message He Is Dead ...' But only in a manner of speaking.

What do we learn from these shared clocks? The full implication of 'broken'. That things no longer work and, oddly enough, that repair is out of the question. There is something odd, something impossible, about the words 'broken' and 'heart' put together. You can't *break* a heart. It isn't a mechanism, in this instance. It is a figure for love. When the heart's mechanism breaks down, we call it heart failure. It is a physical condition. So what do we make of this impossibility – heartbreak?

We learn that heartbreak is hyperbolic – an exaggerated claim to an impossible condition. Those who claim it make exaggerated claims for it. You can hear them raising their voices – so they can shout down the idea of recovery. So others will know what they are suffering. Misery is being acted out.

Finality is being acted out.

But what about the ones who aren't shouting? Who aren't acting the role like Miss Havisham?

People more like Catherine Sloper in *Washington Square*. People whose hearts are invisible.

What is heartbreak, really?

Is it really only rhetoric?

PART I

A Passion for Gardening

Damp Squib Followed by Fireworks

It was 5.30 in the grey morning. Carmen Frazer, who slept lightly, was already dressed. With thickening fingers, she pinched the yellowing leaves from the bottom of the chilli plant on her kitchen windowsill. The plain white saucer had two tartar tidemarks of lime scale and a mascara of grit in the remaining dirty water. Her passion was gardening.

She was 66 and had been retired for seven years. Her sturdy rubber-tipped cherrywood walking stick leaned in the corner. Arthritis of her left hip had made her job at Oxfam impossible: she was co-deputy editor of *JobsWorth*, a small in-house magazine. But the stairs were too difficult. Manoeuvring herself into the car wasn't easy either. She was in constant pain, despite the anti-inflammatories. Toothache the length of her leg, touching a nerve. For her valete in *JobsWorth*, she made a little joke: who put the 'ouch!' in touch? (Colleagues at Oxfam had always found her ready, nervous laugh irritating. Anything – the weather, mention of a queue at the post office – could activate that bright, brief, unconvinced laughter, a door-chime of high soprano, a joke alarm at the lowest setting.)

A second rubber-tipped beechwood outdoor walking stick

stood in the hall. Her walk had a dramatic list to the right as she took the weight off her stiff left leg. To spectators, it looked as if the trouble were in the right leg. As if it were shorter by six inches. Wrong. The hitch was like some South American dance step – a secret weight change in the tango. Except that it wasn't secret. Only misleading.

In 1964 she had taken a boat to Valparaiso. It flew the Liberian flag – easily mistaken for the Stars and Stripes – but was called the *Regina del Mare* and was crewed by Italians mainly, with four Russians who smoked together in the evening – cigarettes with pinched cardboard tubes. It sailed from Liverpool. She was 22. She was going to marry Frank, her fiancé. It was the first and, as it proved, the only time she ever went abroad. The fare, one-way, round Cape Horn, was £275 and fifteen shillings. It included two meals a day. The journey by sea took ten weeks. In that time, she spoke only five words of English: yes, no, please, thank you. Her laugh, she found, was multilingual, a kind of Esperanto. She became familiar with the horizon. She read and then re-read the ten Agatha Christies in her travelling trunk.

When the ship anchored in Montevideo, to provision and take on fuel, at night she heard for the first time the stridulation of insects like an automatic sprinkler system. In the morning, when she walked to the consulate, carefully watching her sandals on the pavement, she glanced up and saw a Negro wearing a stack of panama hats. Maybe twelve. She never forgot the bandoneon of brims, the perfect stutter of hat. There was no mail waiting for her at the consulate.

On the way back, keeping to the shady side of the streets, she saw the bronze scrotum in a bronze church bell. She waited a while, wanting it to strike, staring at the dark metal bruise where it had struck before. Where it always struck. When it struck. But not today, a Saturday.

At the docks, there was a large white ocean-going yacht like a bride. A member of the crew, in white ducks, was leaning out, awkwardly swabbing the white sides with a chamois leather at the end of a long cleft stick – a ginkgo leaf of gold leaf.

How dark her cabin after the aching sunlight, as if she were about to faint. She turned her waistband, undid the zip, stepped out of her skirt and lay on the bunk in her slip. She was trying to think what the sway and the slight bounce of the gangway reminded her of. It came to her. It was like the ship – when it was calm.

At Valparaiso, there was no Frank. There was a messenger who spoke her name as she looked about her, shielding her eyes, her other hand on the green, brass-bound trunk. 'Misshess Carmen Frasseur?'

'Sí.'

He was wearing a double-breasted dark blue suit with sandals. His toenails were dirty. There was an oil stain on his left lapel. His features, though, were handsome. First he showed her a small snapshot of herself – lifting a glass of stout towards the person (Frank) taking the photograph. She was smiling, tensely. Then the messenger held up his left hand, paused, patted his jacket and produced from the inside pocket a letter curved by his ribcage. Then he turned and disappeared between the stacks of dockside crates. No name. The envelope was blank – except for a pastel smudge, franked by the messenger's thumb, which she smelled. Coffee grounds.

Frank's letter was written on lined paper, the top edge a ruffle where it had been torn from a spiral notebook. What it said – that he was sorry, that he had fallen in love with someone else in Chile, another English woman actually, and he had married her – was of no importance. There was no address. But she had his address in her passport and also in her purse. There was a telephone number. She decided not to ring it. Instead, she beckoned a Negro boy with a porter's brass lozenge and paid him to carry her trunk back on to the boat.

The ship was a week in port before it began the return journey of eleven weeks. For some reason, the return journey took a week longer. She had money for the return fare with a goodish sum left over. She had been saving for a long time. In Valparaiso she never left the boat again. She had been on the dockside for ten minutes, including the time it took to read Frank's letter.

On the voyage home, she was, she could tell, a figure of interest, of speculation. Of mystery, in fact. Mainly because she hadn't cried or even looked upset.

She felt insulted and wounded and yet it was a relief.

On the last night in Valparaiso, there was a fireworks display, to celebrate the departure of the plague in 1572 which had claimed 150,000 lives in less than two years. She decided not to watch it. She had seen fireworks before and she wanted to think. The porthole of her cabin bloomed and flickered, tarnished and brightened, like the iris of someone watching fireworks. 'Some bearded meteor, trailing light.' She smiled. She smiled and listened to the bombardment overhead. It lasted thirty minutes and had a surprising dynamic range. The crump of grenades, all grades of ordnance, tracer, tormented shrieks, viciously beaten bass drums, glissandos. A great orchestra of violence, deprived of visual distraction.

She was thinking about the messenger – the way he put his dark glasses over those friendly, handsome eyes, the way he went between the crates, like a pigmy. Or like a giant in Manhattan.

And she came, with a definite jerk, for the first time in her life.

Sharp, then strangely long, like an injection.

Every evening at sea, to the music of Joe Loss on a portable gramophone, she watched two sisters from Slough, in their late thirties, efficiently dancing, breast to breast, on the tiny sloping dance floor. They both worked in the exchange

9

department of Lloyds bank. They had identical wristwatches, equally high on their freckled forearms, and they were going to marry two twin sailors from Valparaiso when they returned in six months' time. They took turns as leader and follower.

———

Here she is at her kitchen table, fingering a jigsaw of thalidomide ginger, thinking about the arthritis in her hands. Her knuckles like bunions, her deviant final finger joints. In the field, beyond the barbed-wire, there are four sheep in their tea cosies that she looks at but doesn't see. She is remembering.

What puzzles her – and what puzzles me – is why she is still attached to a man with whom she was never happy. He hated her laugh and said so. He didn't like the way she smiled. 'Why do you smile like that? As if you're scared.' She held her knife incorrectly at table. They couldn't even talk: 'You interrupt me like your mother.' Everything about her irritated him. Especially in bed. His large penis hurt her. It was a source of resentment (in him) and soreness (in her) that she never came. 'You're supposed to like a big cock.' From the beginning, he found it difficult to come. 'Look, it's like dancing. Why can't you dance?' He was righteous and indefatigable. She suffered constantly from the itching, thrush, and other yeast infections.

No wonder Frank had fallen for someone else.

(Who was equally unhappy.)

And here she was, thinking about him, thinking about his eyes, thinking about the way he thought, the tell-tale compression of his lips, thinking thirty, forty years later, about their lost life together. It would have been misery, but it made no difference. She had given herself, her narrow hips that wouldn't open wide enough at first, her mouth, her hands, the gold-beige, semiprecious hair on her vagina, the vagina itself.

And in return had been given this pendulous body in the big bathroom mirror, gorgonzola dolce, grotesque with gravity, concealed by condensation. In the fog, her upper torso swayed like a bloodhound, nose sampling a spoor.

———

Colin at the garden centre was recovering from cancer of the throat and vocal cords. A silk scarf hid the radical surgical intervention. It wasn't a scar exactly. His neck had gathered round a raw hole, withered like a sick plant. And his voice had changed. It crackled and buzzed like a walkie-talkie.

They were discussing the ginkgo.

'Yea, a.k.a. the Maidenhair tree. Easy to see why. Pretty. Fan-shaped. I don't advise one, Miss Frazer. Since we're old friends. Can grow to be bloody enormous, excuse my Spanish. And the female tree produces a fruit – well, technically, it seeds – that stinks like shit, excuse my Spanish again. So, be warned.'

'Is there a sure way of sexing the sapling?'

'Tricky that. Very tricky.'

She bought a sapling anyway and bedded it down near the barbed-wire fence where two humming birds of polythene blurred in the stiff wind.

PART II

Gallagher and Frazer

I Was So Unfair

The three had spent the hot September afternoon at Garsington Manor, a few miles outside Oxford, the former home of Lady Ottoline Morrell, the literary socialite, whose generosity to artists (the ungrateful D. H. Lawrence, the touchy T. S. Eliot, the snobbish Virginia Woolf) was funded by the brewery fortune – Morrell's Ales – inherited by her husband Philip. He was part of the political world, but tolerated the 'toadies and traitors' – 't-and-t's with their g-and-t's' was his shorthand for his wife's weekend gatherings of guests.

The dovecote blooped and simmered like a pot au feu. They walked between the tall yew hedges down to the lake – a noticeboard of overlapping lily pads, lifted, read, dropped by the fickle wind – and saw the remains of a rowing boat sunk at its mooring. Except for them, the place was deserted. No one had come to the great front door at the end of a deep pebble drive. Noise carried from the brass knocker through the solid oak through the house's ancient wood and tiled acoustic – like a low note struck and impossibly sustained by the pedal held down. But no one answered.

Rex, who knew the current owners of Garsington, wanted

to show the two Americans a ravishing Dufy above the stone mantelpiece in the drawing room.

Gallagher – the poetess was always referred to by her surname – was animated, anxious, voluble. She had the hands and (sandalled) feet of a transsexual but a tiny face whose main feature was a pair of men's horn-rimmed glasses the size of handcuffs. 'It is said,' she was fond of saying, 'that the nose is the only part of the body to grow for the whole of one's life. By the time I die, I hope to have achieved a major nose like Updike's. A significant nose.' Her shrunken head poised on a Brobdingnagian but breastless body, voluminously clad in loose upholstery covers. Ten years later, aged 69, she would die of breast cancer in a matter of two months. And a year later still, Frazer Reid, the tiny law professor she lived with for the last twenty years of her life, would die of breast cancer too.

Her partner, the professor, looked considerably odder than Gallagher. He had prosthetic ears that plugged into his earholes, a precarious arrangement made plausible by his long, implausible Alice Cooper black wig. On windy days, though, the wig was a liability and he would occasionally stoop to pick up an ear. He was without eyebrows or eyelashes, and his features had the abbreviated quality of Down's Syndrome. There were tiny unpredictable oases of facial hair. The red, uneven, shining skin had plastic patches of white fat. It was like *prosciutto crudo* – *'due etti di San Daniele'* – layers of overlapping Parma ham. Frightening – at first. You got used to its surprise surprisingly quickly.

Frazer Reid's voice had the calm of an air-traffic controller's. Its dynamic range just didn't extend to the doubtful, the uneasy, the untoward, the anxious or the excitable. That was Gallagher's speciality.

'Imagine Bertie Lawrence talking to Bertie Russell, Frazer. Talking about the war, I expect. Lawrence was pacifist too, wasn't he? Because of Frieda being a German. Anyway, *on this grass*.'

Frazer smiled with his smudgy mouth. He had learned to put his expressions into his voice. 'Gallagher wouldn't have fitted in here, would you, Gallagher? Them days, you needed a Christian name to be on Christian name terms, even if you had to share it with someone else, some other Bertie.'

'You'd be all right, though. Or maybe you'd be all wrong, come to think of it: your Christian name's a surname.'

———

They were having a pot of Earl Grey when the boy came back from school at five o'clock. He was in the Dragon uniform: grey shirt, grey socks down-gyved, summer sandals and blue corduroy shorts. He was a beautiful, androgynous nine-year-old with quick, brown intelligent eyes and a ready, unguarded grin. He came into the kitchen trailing his satchel on the ground.

'This is Shura,' Rex said. 'Shura, let me introduce you. This is Gallagher. She writes poetry. And this is Frazer, who teaches law in Charlottesville, at the University of Virginia.'

Shura looked directly at Frazer with dazed eyes. 'What happened to your face?'

Rex had never asked. Out of politeness. Now he realised his son had a better idea of politeness.

'I was in an automobile crash. The car caught fire and left my face like this. Actually, worse than this. What you see is a miracle of plastic surgery. I was married to someone who divorced me because of it. I still can't forgive her. How many sentences is that? Five? Six?'

The boy came closer, fascinated, for a better look. His lips were parted. 'What did you look like before?' he asked simply.

'Like this,' Frazer said and took out his wallet, opening it like a cop flashing ID. There was a photograph behind a cellophane window, an image in aspic.

'I can't really see,' the boy said.

Frazer took out the photograph with his awkward fingers and pushed it down the table. 'Consider Phlebas, who was once handsome and tall as you.'

'Who's Phlebas?' the boy asked.

'Someone in a poem by T. S. Eliot.'

'OK,' the boy said absently, 'I know him. Pa's favourite

poet.' He was absorbed in the photograph.

'You look a bit like Eliot, doesn't he, Pa?'

Rex considered. 'Yes, when T. S. E. looked like Tyrone Power. A film star,' he added for the boy's benefit.

The photograph was a photograph of someone else entirely. It bore not the slightest resemblance to Frazer. Why should it? It wasn't a professional studio portrait. It was an imperfectly focused snapshot. The idea of a handsome young man, but no one in particular. Generic. Not Frazer, certainly. Not anyone, actually. This was someone before he was himself. On the cusp. A person on the tip of his own tongue. Both good-looking and featureless.

'Was anyone else in the car?' the boy asked.

'The driver was killed. On impact, apparently. Multiple skull fractures.' Frazer stared at the teapot. 'She was a girl-friend.'

'I didn't know that,' Gallagher said. She took off her spect-acles and began to clean the lenses like a tailor testing material, working it, feeling the weight of the cloth between his fingers.

'That's because I never told you.'

Even the boy could sense a drop in the temperature.

———

I still can't forgive her.

It wasn't the exact truth. It was part of the truth.

It was also true that Shirley, his wife, couldn't forgive him the girlfriend. She felt betrayed. Carol was the friend of them both, a fellow member of the Charlottesville drama club. She directed. They acted. It happened, the affair, when Carol called Frazer in for a line-run.

'Let's start with the beginning of Act II. Want you off-book by Monday. Otherwise you're holding back the rest. And me. I can't get on with the blocking.'

Carol's hair was still damp from the shower. Frazer looked down and was stopped by the dark outline of the nipples under her white T-shirt. She was waiting – and held his gaze when it returned to her face. He started to smile but was stopped again, by the seriousness in her eyes. He thought she was angry. As if he were eight years old and had been caught by his mother going through her purse.

'The art of drama, no, the *essence* of drama is unpredictable inevitability,' she said. 'Watch my lips.' She mouthed something he couldn't understand.

'I don't …'

'Watch my lips,' she repeated. And he watched them move: marginal, significant shifts, gatherings, gives and resistance. Concluding like a wave finally washing the lowest step of a quay with a little flamenco of foam. Again. Her lips executed the exact, incomprehensible ritual again. A message urgent and occult with detail.

'What are you saying?'

'Come closer. Watch my lips.'

He stepped into the whisper of her body odour, beginning to reassert itself in the windowless warmth of the little drama studio.

'I'm not saying anything. I'm making my lips move. Watch my lips.' She took them through the intricate gavotte again, which ended with a moue.

'It's just an exercise I give to actors sometimes. It's nonsense.'

They were magnetically close.

'So is this,' he said and kissed her clamped lips, which after a pause opened to take in his tongue.

'Nonsense? Or an exercise?' she asked when they moved apart.

'Neither. I was being ironical,' Frazer replied. 'Serious and sincere.'

'Or just seduced. By wordless shapes recited in silence – so you have to pay lip-service.'

She was lying. It wasn't a set of abstract shapes. There were words. They were taken from Dickens's *Little Dorrit*. But she never told him, let alone what the words were – Papa, pommes, poules, prunes, prisms – her variant on Mrs General's formula for lending finish to the lips. In fact, she alternated this rigmarole with the original: papa, potatoes, poultry, prunes and prism. The variation was a crucial element of disguise. Of maintaining the mystery. Definitely twins, but twins you could and couldn't tell apart.

She had small, conical, slightly ugly, intriguing breasts. It wasn't the first extramarital affair for either of them.

———

I still can't forgive her.

Frazer preferred the purity of seeing himself as wronged – a man cast out for losing his looks. And anyway, he was ending the affair. That's what caused the crash.

They were parked just off a highway in back of a diner. His Pontiac and her Buick. They were in her car. She was playing with the gear-lever on the steering wheel while he talked. A fidget of semaphore and impatience. The breeze brought a mighty odour of fish from the rubbish containers. Frazer wound up his window.

'It's over, Carol. Sorry. I can't do this to Shirley any more.'

'You mean you don't want to fuck me any more. What *is* that smell? When love congeals / It soon reveals / The faint aroma of performing seals. The great Lorenz Hart. Shirley doesn't know anything about us. So what are you talking about? You can't do this to Shirley any more? Do what?'

'Betray her. Will you stop that with the lever?'

'Fuck you, Frazer.' She drummed her fingers on the rim of the steering wheel instead.

'I love you too much. It's too dangerous.' He was lying. To himself also. He liked being on a high plane – betrayal, remorse, regret. But Carol was right. He was bored by her body. Her sensible, efficient pelvis. Even naked she walked like a tennis player. Her ugly breasts no longer piqued his interest. In retrospect, nothing had been as interesting as their first kiss.

But Carol liked a certain sexual thing he did. It was something he sometimes said. You could never be sure. An insult that excited her. And Frazer knew when to say it. Or when to start saying it. A 'you …' in the right tone of voice at the right moment was on occasion more effective than the completed epithet itself. She found it exciting to imagine her mouth making the two words 'tell me …'

Whereas he was completely unexcited by her, helped to perform by habit, by hitting his marks and taking his cues. The insult was sincere. She knew it was and that was what excited her.

She began to cry.

———

Crying has its own rhetoric. We need a poetics of crying. When we cry, we assume spontaneity, sincerity, because it is a process we cannot control. And yet. Wilfred Owen talks about the eternal reciprocity of tears. This means that someone else's tears create the desire to cry ourselves. It feels natural – because it is – but it shows there is something automatic about tears. A reflex. There is nothing insincere about being tapped on the knee and kicking out. There is nothing insincere about the swallow reflex. But neither comes with the moral commendation that tears automatically accrue. Tears come with a non-negotiable, fixed-rate, moral currency – as do Hitler (negatively) and Shakespeare (positively). Of course, we know that Shakespeare's plays aren't uniformly excellent (*Pericles*, *Two Gentlemen of Verona* – though you can always find an academic willing to advance the merit of either), but he is, *nevertheless*, a genius. Tears are a way of winning the argument. They are a physical manifestation over which we have no control. They are like diarrhoea. And no one has *ever* suggested, even for an explosive second, that diarrhoea is insincere or contrived.

But no one has suggested either that there is a positive moral dimension to diarrhoea.

Behind the idea of sentimentality is our sense that the emotion felt by us hasn't been 'earned'. That we have cried too readily. 'Sentimentality' registers our sense of the automatic. 'Unearned': we haven't done the work, put in the effort; we have profited from a reflex.

Sometimes, we are moved by being moved. Two emotions – both genuine – yet the second is a significant qualification. Most of us, however, consider the two emotions as one augmented emotion.

If we can't control crying, we should consider the possibility that it controls us. During an illness, this is called the Cascade Effect. Something minor causes the blood pressure to drop dramatically, which affects the heart, which affects the lungs, which affects the liver …

Which can kill us, quite quickly, from a standing start.

It was going to kill Carol.

When Carol started to cry, she was gripped by the Cascade Effect. By the rhetoric of her tears. A mild sadness, not unmixed with irritation, actually – 'Fuck you, Frazer' – quickly escalated into the tragic.

Or the hysterical.

She hadn't realised how much she cared.

She hadn't known how much she cared.

———

Not that much, in fact. But it made no difference. She felt an ice-cream ache in her soft palate. Her mouth opened and tears gathered along her eyelids. Silently as flood waters finding their way, almost intelligently. She was trying not to blink, to keep the tears at bay. The surface tension held, held

– and then broke. Water spilled down her face. A toad shifted its weight in her revolted mouth. She took a quick noisy breath. Another. And then the tears jumped. She was winded, unable to get her breath. As if Frazer had hit her in the stomach. She couldn't speak. She was drowning before his eyes.

Afraid, he got out of the car.

As she heard the door slam, she put the car into 'drive' and her foot on the gas pedal, right down to the worn carpet, taking the Buick on to the highway in front of the diner. It was a miracle she got so far. She could see nothing.

A pick-up going in the same direction took out the Buick, which sheared off a road sign with its side mirror and rico-cheted back into the traffic, where it was hit by a Standard Oil gas-tanker and crushed against the concrete divider. Frazer ran to the wreck. As he was trying to work her (dead) body free, the gas-tanker exploded. Trees evapo-rated instantly, metal deformed itself trying to escape, the road itself was on fire.

He was lucky to survive.

Or unlucky.

———

I still can't forgive her.

It is true he hadn't forgiven her. Nor could he forget her. He couldn't forgive her partly because he still loved her. Even though Shirley had been dead for a decade. A skiing fatality: she was hit on the slopes by a snowboarder intent on showing off by going at speed through the narrowest of gaps between her and a friend. At the last moment, she leaned fatally forward. Her protective helmet made it hard to hear. The friend was left paralysed from the waist down. The 16-year-old snowboarder broke his leading left leg in two places.

Loving the dead. The rich silt of memories.

Shirley ate Phillips' Milk of Magnesia tablets as if they were sweets. She shook the dark blue bottle gleefully like maracas. He could still see the coating, the whitewash, left on her long tongue.

She bit her fingernails as she read. Snicks. Painful, satisfying tearings, with which she picked her teeth. Her tongue played with pieces wedged between her front teeth. Each quick was bared, a frayed frontier of pink, the grip-seal on a plastic bag, a gap, a gash, recovering cosmetic surgery.

(How many epithets is that? Count the commas. A handful. Five.)

Her immortal, pizza-crust, spatulate finger-ends. In his mind, still unable to pick up a pin with ease.

The beautiful blot of her arsehole. A dark-pink peach-stone. An astonishment of lips.

Her laugh. The way she smoked before she gave up. Smoke trickling up her nostrils. Spokes of smoke when she spoke.

Whenever Frazer thought about her, he was his own raw quick, both pained and pleasured, unforgiving and unhealed, unable to help himself, unable to stop.

Odd, isn't it, how his impaired present inserts itself into these memories? Frazer went on loving his wife because then he was still himself. His love was continuous with his old self. When he was beautiful, before he was burned.

————

He had never loved Gallagher. He could see she was kind and he liked her well enough when she wasn't being irritating. Which, however, was most of the time. He found her body irritating. The big-boned, ultra-pelvic Henry Moore torso and the midget Henry Moore head – that deliberate, synthetic pseudo-modernist mismatch. Moore irritated him too.

Frazer sometimes said that he was a much nicer person since his face was burned. It wasn't true. It is hardly ever true that tragedy does anything other than deform us, when it doesn't destroy us completely.

So much for Nietzsche: what doesn't destroy me makes me more irritable.

One day he said to Gallagher they should convert and join

the Taliban. 'Just saw a woman wearing a bur'qa – looking out through her mail-slot.' He paused, maliciously. 'We could both benefit from the dress-code.'

Gamely, Gallagher laughed.

How did they come to be together? After all, Frazer didn't go out much – beyond giving his lectures and classes. They met in the rolling stacks of the Law Library holdings. Gallagher, poet in residence for the year at Charlottesville, was tired of being teased by Irvin Ehrenpreis, the professor who had sponsored her for the post. He was better read in contemporary poetry than her and, discovering this, was delighted to discuss his latest finds. 'Is it focus or fear that makes you ignore Straus Galassi?' Irvin would ask over coffee, grey eyes lit with mischief.

(There was no such poet. Ehrenpreis had made him up – and could quote quite a lot of his 'Boston Antiphon' – 'Surely a major work?' There was something about Gallagher – the seriousness of her spectacles, probably – that encouraged downright deception.)

So she took to having her books sent across to the Law Library. Collecting them from the Main Desk, she took them to the windowless stacks – where she couldn't be spotted, hiding from Ehrenpreis, by Ehrenpreis.

One day, she dropped her armful of books when Frazer's

face appeared from between LJ6: 88.00–280.00 and LJ7: 280.01–400.00. LJ was Dewey for Law Journals.

Just then, she couldn't remember if she'd screamed or not. Her hands went to her ears like the Munch. He looked like a lizard – a salamander, actually, in navy-blue suspenders and a Brooks Brothers shirt.

'I'm sorry,' Gallagher said. 'You frightened me.'

'The effect I generally have,' Frazer said. And he smiled his difficult smile. 'Sometimes people scream. They do. Thank you for not screaming. My position is academically precarious enough without a sexual impropriety charge. Unlikely as that may seem in this unlikely context: apparently libido flourishes in libraries. Especially in the rolling stacks. Propinquity creates its own pressures.'

Apart from that semester's lectures on Tort, Frazer hadn't said so much in months.

He invited her for a cocktail, gave her his campus address, knowing it was an offer she couldn't refuse.

Propinquity creates its own pressures. They had almost touched. Contact was forced on them.

She came.

———

He liked the way Gallagher was slightly grotesque. It

answered a preference he didn't know he had till then. True, he had been taken by the bubblegum bulge of Carol's nipples – asymmetric hernias – but it wasn't that. He still loved female physical beauty: that fold in dough, the clean, incomplete crease in the rounded top of a woman's thigh, was painful to him. The thought of it constricted his breathing. It was more potent than pornography, which he disdained – for its narrow focus and also because it was impossible for him to purchase inconspicuously. Even by post: those flagrantly nondescript manila envelopes. He loved beauty more than ever, more even than the compelling ugliness of genitals. So it wasn't a perversion, this new preference. Rather that he preferred to keep company with the disadvantaged.

We surprise ourselves more obviously as we grow older. But at every age there are always bits of ourselves that are hidden from ourselves. I don't mean shameful things that we conceal from others and ourselves – though there are plenty of those. I mean, for example, discovering that we dislike some of our oldest friends – a realisation generally brought about by *their* antipathy being made manifest. You make an innocent, unconsidered remark – the kind of remark you make among friends – and one of your friends, of whom you have an affectionately low opinion, holds it up for scrutiny and friendly ridicule. When this happens with increasing frequency, you start putting inverted commas around 'friendly'. Or you have a success – which your friend humorously disparages. (Oscar Wilde in 'The Soul of Man

Under Socialism': 'it requires a very fine nature ... to sympathise with a friend's success.') You discover, gradually, a desire to hurt, to retaliate, to wound, which is primitive and demeaning.

You tell yourself, be realistic, for godsake. No friendship, you say, consists of unalloyed mutual admiration. Why should it? And yet the problem isn't that friendship should be uncritical and supportive – and isn't quite. It is that friendship is a form of competitive condescension – masked and improved by the myth of itself.

Defenders of friendship are vocal. They are the friends who tell you how much they disliked the work of other friends. And ask you not to pass it on. Friendship is one friend betraying another friend to a third friend. With a fond, friendly smile. The greater the betrayal, the greater the intimacy – the greater the friendship.

Another surprise – discovering that none of this is incompatible with genuine warmth and real affection.

———

Gallagher and Frazer sat in deckchairs, drinking margaritas out of jam jars. The uncut grass was a foot and a half, two feet high. 'I prefer nature to the garden,' Frazer explained. 'It's my romantic temperament. And it renders me invisible.'

Gallagher thought: it's like talking to ET. You forget he

looks like a scalded cockroach. She said, prodding the bridge of her spectacles, '"The Mower, Against Gardens". A poem by Marvell.'

'Was he a romantic?'

'Not officially. About two hundred years too old. So I'd say, a very elderly romantic. He wrote "To His Coy Mistress" and that's famously romantic. Seize the day.'

'Sleaze the day, huh. A dirty poem, I assume?' (Frazer knew the poem from high school, in fact. Of course he did.)

Gallagher gradually fell in love with him. He could make her laugh. One oppressively hot July afternoon, Frazer was fanning her vigorously, with a small piece of cardboard awkwardly gripped. 'I find it quite difficult to bring a woman to orgasm using this method,' he said, expressionlessly, after persevering for a couple of minutes. 'But I'm up for it if you are. Shall we continue? You have to work at these things.'

When she stopped laughing, he added: 'You old slyboots, you just had a multiple disguised as a giggle. But you can't fool Frazer. He knows when he has a woman in his grip.'

And it was true. He did know.

———

Before she did, in fact.

His references, his playful references, to sex increased. It was a form of wooing that would have been a little creepy in a normal man. But his features granted Frazer amnesty. The remarks could only be ironic with a face like that.

As well as being a poet, Gallagher was also a singer-composer. She had written quasi-jazz settings, atonal bebop, for some Shakespeare songs and sonnets. She asked Frazer did he think it was OK to print Shakespeare's words amended? Spelling, for instance, 'vats' for 'phats', 'would' for 'should'.

He replied: 'Of course. Shakespeare's only a fucking poet for God's sake.' His lawyer's ready contempt. An error instantly retrieved: 'He should be so lucky – to spend five minutes in your mouth.'

In your mouth. Her pout raised above the office of poet. He was forgiven and Gallagher flattered.

———

In the end, Gallagher had to ask Frazer if she could kiss him. Not the other way round. There was no possibility that Frazer would ever risk rejection, however certain he might be of the outcome.

They had never touched. Not even accidentally. Not even brushed against each other in a confined space. The nearest they had come to touching was in the Law Library stacks.

Frazer carried himself warily, like someone just out of intensive care, only half healed, after months of dressings, unforgettable as final unction. Gallagher wondered what his skin felt like when it was touched – to him and by her. He looked so sore. And yet, as it proved, he was oddly thick-skinned and felt very little. 'I am awaiting the return of the nerves to the epidermis. They're being pretty damned slow about it. It's sort of like being a leper, I imagine. Except that lepers are traditionally silver and I'm more (wouldn't you say) Thermidor. And I know better than they did to be careful of my precious nose.'

One wet November evening, translating and clarifying as she went, Gallagher risked reading Frazer *The Testament of Cresseid* by Henryson. At the end of the poem, when Cresseid has leprosy, she and Troilus meet – without either recognising the other. Frazer was moved. He held up his claw hand – to stop her and to hide his face. He was thinking of himself and Shirley. She had not recognised *him*. Deliberately.

Frazer's unchangeable face changed underneath itself, unmistakably. Salt water stood shining in the red rim of his eyelid like mercury in a thermometer. Hard to see, clear. Visible, invisible. His smile was even stranger, less convincing than usual.

'Would it be OK if I kissed you?' Gallagher asked. 'I would like to kiss you. On the mouth, if that's OK.'

'If you must, I suppose you must.' The tone was curmudgeonly, but he was smiling the old crooked smile again. Not the stricken version. 'It usually comes to this with girls.'

Frazer's face, his entire body, felt like soft glove leather – thin smooth kid – in uneven layers.

Only his penis was perfectly normal. Served by all the necessary nerves. Saved by some miracle of retraction.

But penises feel like glove leather anyway.

———

They were in bed. Her surreal glasses loomed like an observatory on the bedside table.

'I used to be a lesbian. In my twenties and thirties,' Gallagher told him. 'I had short hair in those days.'

Now her centre-parted grey hair hung in long bohemian skeins. She hadn't been to a hairdresser in years. ('Not since 1964, actually.') It was a style too young for her – just as Patti Smith is too old to go on looking like Patti Smith.

'I used to go to these dyke bars.'

'Thought you couldn't say "dyke" any more,' Frazer said.

'That's what we called them then, that's all I can say. But maybe we were appropriating the insult. Tell the truth, I don't remember.'

She drew up her knees and stared at the past.

'It was before I got started in with poetry. I was in the arts sort of in a general way: I was interested in video art and opera. I guess that's how come the singing now. I was assistant director of a thing at Houston Opera. Round about 1970 or thereabouts.'

'So, are you still basically a lesbian?' Frazer asked. 'Can I ask you that?'

'It's never seemed important. You know. As long as I love people, it's never seemed important how their genitals happen to be configured.'

Two things occurred to Frazer. That was why she didn't care about his burned exterior. It was like colour-blind casting in the theatre. It genuinely didn't bother some people. Second, there was something crucial missing in her sexuality – a compelling preference, a categorical imperative, an undeniable reflex. Something to serve slavishly or violate perversely. Gallagher was without perversity. She was less than innocent; she was sexually stupid.

This mattered more to him than her strange ungainly body, the pelvis like a snake that has swallowed a picture frame.

———

You see, he wasn't very nice. Frazer was too intelligent and too honest to be completely nice. But he worked at it and he became known for his niceness. He would sometimes describe himself as 'the notoriously nice Frazer Reid' – and add, 'Don't you believe it.' But everyone did.

On campus, they became known as an item, a couple. The kids thought they were cute. Addams Family, sure, but cute. They were an advert for the power of love. 'It's like the Prioress in Chaucer last semester: in the Prologue, the like Latin motto *amor vincit omnia*. You think it's kinda gross, but it just isn't at all. I think they're safe.'

In the late nineties Gallagher had a great, unexpected success. She won a Pulitzer prize for *Way Out West*, a collection of poems about growing up in Texas. 'Stetson' was a particular popular favourite after the President credited, quoted and enacted its first line at a televised press conference on his ranch – beating the indestructible dust off of a stetson against his leather chaps.

Gallagher's face – and glasses – made the cover of *Time* magazine. (*Newsweek* pulled their interview when the cover appeared.) She fitted a treasured American type: the lovable, eccentric poetess, a role that had been free since the death of Marianne Moore. Her Franciscan sandals and her big bare feet were the subject of affectionate joshing on *Letterman*. When Gallagher appeared on *The Daily Show*, Jon Stewart produced a pair of identical glasses from a drawer and wore them for the duration of the interview.

Even Ehrenpreis, had he still been alive, would have had to stop teasing her. (Or would he?) Frazer retired behind her celebrity. He was loyal and especially supportive when a snippy notice appeared. The *New Yorker* ran a profile in which various acquaintances from the video world spoke of her egoism and her humourlessness. She was quoted as saying, 'I don't want to be famous for my sandals' and 'I'm more than a pair of glasses.' She also said that celebrity could be 'irksome'. It was the inflection of jokiness in the public regard that she didn't like. But she thought it was celebrity itself. Her belated elegy, 'John Lennon', was dismissed as self-indulgent, a hubristic, gratuitous, unearned act of identification. (She praised his misunderstood, his questing, art, and identified Mark David Chapman as someone unable to distinguish seer from celebrity.)

Frazer was full of good advice. Be calm. Relax. Smile more. It isn't the Gettysburg Address. It's the most popular TV show ever, so what's wrong with being on *The Simpsons*? Lighten up.

Privately he thought: interesting, she's being burned in the blast furnace of publicity. Touchy. Thin-skinned. Longing to be someone else, somewhere else.

Gallagher's hunger for high seriousness was eased by her induction into the American Academy of Arts and Sciences. Frazer couldn't imagine her now, even in private, making a joke about wanting a substantial, a Library of America nose.

———

She didn't seem to be writing much either.

When Rex visited her in New York, she was planning a theatre project. (Frazer had taken a post at Columbia, partly because Gallagher was attracted to the anonymity of Manhattan.) She talked for three hours about Henry Crabb Robinson and his relationship with the Wordsworths. 'See, Crabb Robinson is the peripheral figure who brings the principals together in the play. I figure he can narrate and he can participate.' Hardly anyone else spoke. Frazer kept the glasses filled.

The other guest was a German opera director. Outside, he turned to Rex as they looked about for cabs, and said in his excellent English: 'Thank God, I'm not a theatre director. Can I give you a lift anywhere? I'm going to Fifth and 21st. No? Well, good night.'

As he folded his long frame into the cab, he added, 'Do you think she's mad? Or just hyper? A play about Crabb Robinson? *Now?* After Beckett?'

'Wasn't Beckett's first play about Samuel Johnson?' Rex shouted as the cab door slammed.

Then the window wound down. 'She might as well call it *Wikipedia – The Play.*'

It was beginning to snow and Rex had a couple of blocks to walk before his hotel. The street spooks tottered and fawned. The stars fell and kept on falling. Rex was a tiny bit drunk.

Gallagher was writing more than people thought – some of her best work, all of it unpublishable.

Around this time, roughly 1995, maybe earlier, Gallagher fell in love with someone else – the choirmaster of a Roman Catholic cathedral in Midtown. Every week-day at noon, she entered its dusk to listen to the music practice. There was something priestly about him, though he wasn't a priest. It might have been his stillness. Except that priests were never still – their glossy garments sweeping through the nave like Cyd Charisse, genuflecting, hand jiving, twirling, auditioning, performing, busy. The choirmaster had stage presence too, if a less advertised form. Gallagher couldn't not look at him. He raised his hands. He was still. For two seconds only. And then the music was his hands.

He was making music – Howells, Finzi, Holst – so you could see the sounds in the serried air.

Serried. Then just as suddenly empty when his sound-proof right hand closed off the notes.

Difficult delight, simple sorrow, then deafness. Silence and the memory of music.

He recognised her. 'Aren't you Gallagher? The poet? Saw you on *Letterman*.'

'I never went on *Letterman*. I was on *The Daily Show*. And

41

Larry King Live.' She laughed. '*That* was a mistake. You didn't see that, did you?'

He shook his head.

'*Good.*'

It was the first time for a long time that she felt grateful for celebrity.

'You come here practically every day.'

'Yea, well, I'm in love with English church music,' she explained, quietly overjoyed to have used the words 'in love'.

He smiled. 'We do a fair bit of Poulenc too. And Fauré as well.'

'I know,' she said. 'I love that stuff too.' She was grinning inexplicably. 'Buy you a coffee?'

'That would be nice,' he said. 'There's a cafeteria in the basement. We could go there.'

In a brown, curly-brimmed Parisian bowler, he would have looked like Edgar Degas. A strong dark beard closely shaven, hair the colour of burnished steel, a straight nose and full dark lips. A serious, Scottish face that didn't laugh readily, whose ironical brown eyes looked straight at you. Perhaps he was 55.

Gallagher looked down at his magic hands, tanned and tufted, as they rested modestly, incognito, on the table, disguised as servants, having carried two cups across the cafeteria to this corner. This corner where they met most days after practice, taking turns to pay. He and his hands had a quality of containment that drew her in. The fingers flexed and it was like an irresistible argument, forceful, objective, logical.

He was tall, slim, grey, gifted and definitely handsome. His name was Rupert Cockburn. 'Pronounced "Co'burn", but actually spelled "Cockburn". Appropriately enough, I guess.'

It was several months before he explained the appropriateness.

———————

There *was* something priestly about him. He'd been a Jesuit but left the Order so he could marry. After a few years of happiness, he discovered he was gay, so was now a celibate once again. He thought homosexuality was obviously a sin. 'God can forgive me, He doesn't have to agree with me. I have to agree with Him, wouldn't you say? Why should He suddenly, conveniently change His mind at the end of the twentieth century? I'm with W. H. Auden on this one.'

Gallagher managed not to tell him that, when she was in love with someone, she had no sexual or genital preference.

She managed not to tell him either that she loved him. Out of loyalty to Frazer, to disfigured, loyal, long-suffering Frazer. Grateful, long-suffering Frazer whom she had irritated for twenty years, who couldn't bear the smell she left in the can, so great was his antipathy by now.

She wrote a poem about Frazer – after a solitary holiday in Tuscany – a prose poem called 'Lizard'. She decided not to dedicate it to him. That would make the connection too obvious. Then she decided not to publish it at all: she didn't want to hurt his feelings with the title. So the dedication, now harmless, was restored. After the title, there wasn't anything he should mind.

Lizard

I've just seen a lovely thing. I was about to do the dishes after my siesta. I noticed a movement in the sink among the cups and coffee grounds. A little lizard that couldn't get up the porcelain. Next to the chain of the plug. It stopped in mid-shimmy as soon as it felt my eyes on it. I caught it carefully in a glass. It was quite still so I didn't damage it. I suppose it was about four inches long, but the body not much over an inch. It was all tail. And its legs ended with those bent-wire horsefly fingers. I can see why jewelers use them so much, but jewelry is so much less elegant than the real thing. Their leather suits are miniaturised and fit them perfectly. Subtle but distinct patterns. Like the chasing on an arquebus. And a Teflon quality that is heavenly: there it was, untouched by the grounds and the grease, straight from the tailor in an outfit worn only once. And when I tipped it out into the garden, it stayed still, except for the pulse of the lungs, and then it made off, immaculate, a dandy through the dirt.

When Frazer read it and the dedication, after her death, he thought it had nothing to do with him – except the insulting, inaccurate equation of him and the lizard. The good-looking lizard. He was affronted by the flattery, resented the coarse compassion. He preferred to be his horrific authentic self in print. Gallagher was too bourgeois, too bien pensant, to tell the fucking truth. She'd got the lizard, though. He removed the dedication and sent the prose poem to Wendy Lesser at *The Threepenny Review.*

Gallagher also left behind two sonnet sequences – one about her life with Frazer, which he hated, though he could see it wasn't bad poetry. He saw things differently, that's all. *She* felt trapped. By her goodness. What about *him*? He had his own point of view, which disagreed with hers. So he destroyed the sequence. Fuck *her.* And since he knew Gallagher wasn't one of the poetic greats – he was right – he felt no particular guilt.

The second sonnet sequence was about the choirmaster. Frazer was genuinely surprised, he had such a low opinion of Gallagher's powers of attraction. The sequence was one of her best things. It captured the strange joy of heartbreak and the perpetual surprise of music, even known, loved music. Both had that held-breath feeling just before blackout. Music and being in love were always new. The pain of heartbreak seemed a small price to pay for this perpetual ache of unsatisfied joy – this impossible note sustained at the height of heaven.

Shirley.

Frazer gave the sequence to the Gallagher Archive at the University of Virginia Library, Charlottesville, with an embargo on publication and quotation till 2030, though accredited scholars could consult the manuscript. Frazer thought the genuine merits of the sequence might be magnified by report. The embargo was a calculated act of shrewd career management.

———

On the day she died, in Bethesda Hospital, on the fortieth floor, she never recovered consciousness. Frazer listened to the shallow slur of her breath, and remembered one of Gallagher's lines: 'a child asleep, understudying the ocean.' Her big hand lay open, supine on the sheet. An IV drip was taped into her bruised arm. The air conditioning breathed noisily in unison. Outside, the late July evening basted the city.

Then as Frazer watched, the heart monitor suddenly flat-lined. It had taken a week to settle the phosphorescence, the seethe and tangle, of heartbeats and smooth out that incoming tide. A week that felt like a long walk without food. Frazer's legs ached. He was hungry. Or empty. He didn't know which.

Miroslav Holub

The last time I saw him in London, the poet Holub had aged and walked with a dislocation. His cheap white summer shoes had marshmallow soles. He was wearing a light blue blazer with brass buttons and grey slacks. He looked like an impostor, a foreign spy at the Henley Regatta. Or just an old man. My father dressed like that in his eighties – the dress code of those approaching death.

The jerky, impeded walk of a man stuck in a turnstile, admitted, and stuck in a turnstile, admitted, and stuck in a turnstile. He said it was rheumatoid arthritis. It looked as likely to be cancer of the prostate metastasising to his hips.

It was the last time I saw him.

He had the uneven wide thin lips of an alligator who has remembered a joke and is wondering whether to tell it. After his death, there was talk of his being an informer. Earlier, a Czech exile in America accused Holub of similar treachery, but later withdrew the charges. His name must be in my notebooks.

It is certainly true that Holub's translator, Ian Milner, talked to the Prague secret police. Milner was a New Zealander and a Communist sympathiser who had gone to

Prague in the fifties and married a Czech, Jarmila, a woman whose beauty still felt potent in her late seventies. The myth of our attractiveness survives its destruction.

Either Milner reported or was deported. He had no choice. He was in love. So his heart was broken in a different way – slowly. He died of cancer of the ear. (The informer's appropriate site, you could say – but only if you had no heart to break.)

I don't suppose he told the Castle anything other than low-quality, minor gossip: 'Had lunch with Holub. Seems depressed. Hasn't written much recently.' He was amiable, attentive, slightly boring, partly because he was hard of hearing. I think I remember cotton wool, pellets stained with oil of camphor, in his ears – one of which would kill him.

Holub had the mouth of someone who knows he will be asked to inform in exchange for permission to travel to the USA, to Oberlin College, where his American mistress lived. I prefer to think of this as a transaction rather than as treachery – a transaction with a fluctuating rate of exchange. In return for hard foreign currency, fiduciary fraud – small amounts of *korunas*, invalid except in Comecon countries.

You don't take a stand. You make a calculation. You decide to play the game, to gamble and cheat.

(Only editorial writers take a stand. The rest of us – you and I – we take a risk.)

Holub also had the mouth of someone who had left the only woman he really loved. The mouth of a man who has made a mistake.

I spent sixteen hours on a train with Holub from Bhopal to New Dehli in 1989. We were part of a poetry festival. On the train, he talked about his two children, a boy and a girl, aged 7 and 9. I would have guessed that Holub was 62 – old to have such young children. In all the artificial, sincere intimacy of the long shared journey, I asked Holub if he had married late. On the other hand, I added, he struck me as the very opposite of the philandering poet figure – who remains unmarried in an ecstasy of promiscuity, ceaselessly gratified by groupies and starfuckers.

He explained: 'For me, sex is impossible without love. So I told myself I was in love and divorced my wife. Then I married again. The new woman. It was a mistake. The woman I really loved was my first wife.'

The boy and the girl were by the second wife. He had a son, much older, by the first.

A mistake made by love. A mistake made by desire. A mistake made with good intentions by a good man.

This mouth, those thin lips, are what it sometimes means to have a broken heart.

PART III

Annunciata Williams-McCrae

By Design

They had a long list of fancy names for girls, many of them foreign, as well as a shorter list of traditional English names for boys. George, Arthur, William, John, Albert, Henry, Charles. Annunciata was the girl's name they decided on before she was born. After she was born, unsurprisingly, she was known as Annie. Had she been a boy, she would have been Edward.

She had Down's Syndrome.

———

Hamish McCrae, a scion of Harrow and before that a prep school in Suffolk, had never had a Scottish accent. In fact, his parents, a musical couple, had moved, early in their marriage, from Lossiemouth in Morayshire and settled in Aldeburgh, where they cleaned, cooked and managed the Red House and the Red Studio for Benjamin Britten and Peter Pears. Britten, taken by the boy's extraordinary beauty, had paid for the prep school and the fees for Harrow.

The boy's beauty was interesting – so much depended on the marginal, on the tiniest touches, nothing in themselves, that together somehow transfigured the whole.

For example, Britten's wavy hair had the coarse, springy texture of a chow. There was a copper-wire quality and a regularity that made it look artificial, especially after a visit to the barber, when it looked like a wig. Hard-wearing, waterproof hair for everyday use. Harris tweed for the head.

Whereas Hamish's hair was a rich, glossy mahogany with even darker chestnut tones the colour of bitter chocolate. It wasn't curly; the waves and whorls were too relaxed for that. Nor was it straight. The word 'locks' was invented for Hamish's hair. They swung, they tangled, they curved, they touched, they thickened, they hung out together. They were 'unruly', they required a hand to relish and discipline their delightful disorder, their irrepressible spring.

The blue eyes and the blackness of the lashes. Not the expected contrast of a pale, washed-out turquoise denim against black. Rather an intensification of colour. The blue was a dark midnight, a navy-blue, infinitesimally lighter than the pupil. The eyelashes opened and gathered like the mascara-ed stamens in a tulip. The eyeballs were at once very white and influenced by the irises.

His features were straight, handsome, almost unemphatic, though in adolescence they took on character. It was the expression in the face – the slightly parted lips, a way of looking through you towards some perpetual mild surprise – that caught at the heart and held it.

Hamish sometimes imagined that his life – the warm freckled eggs in the bald mud nest, the tiny pale blue eggs in the sparrow's angora bonnet, the jackpot pebbles under your feet at Aldeburgh, the way without thinking you just hit a note by thinking your voice there – he sometimes imagined that all this was delusion, that he was laid in a coma, dreaming detail that would just disappear, replaced by something infinitely duller. It lent his eyes, his whole face, a look of wary wonder that made Britten fall in love with the boy – treasure the insignificant, meaningless touch of those slim tanned hands.

And of course, the boy was right. He *was* living in a coma, as he later discovered.

———

Hamish decided not to go to Oxford, or Cambridge, or any other university. He wanted to be a reporter, not even a 'journalist'. With his first wages from the *Bath and Wells Argus*, he splashed out on a trench-coat and felt like a lead in *The Front Page*. By now he knew he was handsome. Later he would joke that at Harrow he was the school cert. He wasn't. But older boys liked to touch him, take him by the wrist, tell him to wash his filthy hands. One or two of the sixth formers would watch him over their books as they revised for their A-levels outdoors. It was like being a royal. He was used to being special, watched. Without being self-conscious, he was always conscious of his self, knowing he was noticed. He could never be invisible.

By now, he expected to be liked and he was. His looks, however, created a kind of passivity. There was no reason to go out of his way: a charm offensive would have been offensive and unnecessary. But it meant that girls were never in contention. Hamish didn't know how to pursue them, how to make the going. He smiled. They melted. Nothing happened.

So it was that he married Lucinda, a slightly gawky aristocrat, the second daughter of an earl with land in Ireland. She was confident enough – with her gold tooth and her tiny tattoo and her inaudible delivery – to pick him and choose him. Hamish, it has to be said, was a snob too – the result of his Scottish parents, their domestic employment, and their displacement as mentors by Britten and Pears. Hamish appreciated their social disadvantage.

Lucinda wrote cookery books for a living, two a year to begin with, appeared on television and picked up a nickname in *Private Eye:* Prunier Shears, the Lady Trug. Hamish migrated from Bath to London, where he worked for the *Sunday Times* on the 'comic', the colour supplement. He and Lucinda were an item. Photographers papped them when they arrived at parties.

The marriage, however, didn't last. After ten years Hamish moved out of Cheyne Walk into a bachelor flat further along the Thames. He discovered Lucinda had been having an affair for at least five years with the producer of her television series. Hamish was shocked – Alan, the producer, had a chipped front tooth, a Real Ale belly and more than one unshaven chin. When Lucinda launched counter-accusations of infidelity – what about your fucking affairs, if it comes to that? – Hamish explained he had never slept with anyone else.

She didn't believe him.

Francesca was the designer daughter of two designer parents. She was a colleague on the comic and had designs on Hamish, now he was officially free. She was ten years younger than him.

As a 17-year-old at art school (Central Saint Martins) she had moved in with Luke Pritchard, who was 50 and the founder of Bespoke Earplug, or B. E., the design group with offices in Knightsbridge, Fifth Avenue, Singel 2, Montmartre, Charlottenburg and La Giudecca (next to the old Fortuny factory). It was Francesca who gave him the nickname Lucky. 'A design coup. The designer designed. Well, definitely re-branded. And you *are* lucky at your age, bloody lucky, to be having nooky with a slip like me.' He knew he was. He also knew his luck wouldn't last.

The relationship lasted till his 55th birthday and her 22nd. The split was her present to herself. Five years seemed long enough to Francesca, even though Lucky still had the worn, scuffed charm of a 48 Hasselblad. She wanted to marry and marry a husband 'with legs for the long haul'. She was a woman who knew her mind. She moved out as efficiently as she had moved in. After one or two rages, drunk late-night visits, six or seven sympathy fucks ('I don't fucking *want* a sympathy fuck'), Lucky managed to disguise his disappointment.

Francesca was now in her early twenties and built like a boy. Her short dark hair had a side parting. Her arms were lithe and muscular and faintly hairy below her rolled-up shirt sleeves. In all this androgyny – narrow hips and pelvis, breasts that were nothing but nipple – her high buttocks were surprisingly steatopygous. She wore grey school shirts to mid-thigh, cinched with a snake belt and topped with one of her collection of old school ties. She kept a catapult in her satchel and described it as 'a twig with an eye-patch' to a police constable who wondered whether it constituted an offensive weapon. To strangers in the street who stared, she put her head on one side and said, 'Who's a pretty boy, then?'

But it was the ties that attracted Hamish's attention. 'That's a Harrow tie you're wearing, did you know that?'

'Pull, pull together,' she sang and lit a roll-up with her Zippo. 'Expect there was quite a lot of that – pulling together – on the river,' she paused fractionally, 'in the dorms.'

'Wrong school. That's the Eton Boating Song. And it's "*Swing, swing* together".'

They were married in three months. She married him. 'I want to be your bum boy,' was the way she proposed. 'You've awakened my dormant bisexuality,' was the way, with an elaborately theatrical yawn, Hamish accepted.

Did I say that her face was beautiful?

————

It was three years, four expensive Wigmore Street consultations, strictly observed practice of best practice in bed and two courses of fertility treatment before Francesca was jubilantly pregnant. 'Hamish. Hamish.' He looked up from his paper across the breakfast things. They were in the tiny conservatory.

'What?'

'Tits. I'm getting tits. Look at my new tits.' She pulled open her dressing gown.

Hamish looked over his half-moon reading glasses. 'Good for you. Or should that be, good for me? What an exciting development. Though rather at the planning stage, I'd say.'

'Fuck you. I've always wanted to know what it felt like to have tits.'

'Very soon, you may have the vaguest idea.'

'Fuck fuck *you*.'

'There seems to be another side effect as well. Am I imagining this, or is your fanny more – how can I put this indelicate matter delicately? – even more hirsute than formerly, if that is physically possible?'

Francesca's fanny was a glorious irrepressible Afro pompon ('to go with my Botswana bottom'). She looked down and hmmmed.

'De dark incontinent, massa Hamish. Yo sexplorer dis mornin? Or do you have to get into work for something urgent?'

'I can feel the weight of my solar topee.'

————

The young, balding doctor, another Hamish, was open and friendly. He sat back in his Fair Isle pullover, smiling, his hands locked behind his head. (As she spread the cold KY on her bump, the nurse had told Francesca he was known in the unit as 'Mighty Mouse' because of his skill with the ultrasound remote.)

'Nothing to worry about there. No surprises, I'd say. All the measurements add up satisfactorily. Soooo, first things first: would you like to know the sex of your baby?'

They answered almost together.

'Yes.'

'No.'

Francesca looked at her Hamish – who dolefully revised his answer. 'No.'

'We'd prefer a surprise,' Francesca said. 'He's just being naughty, aren't you?'

'Fine,' the doctor said. 'Don't understand it myself, but folks often opt not to know. Let me explain a bit about the sonograph and what it can check for. OK. Basically, it translates the reflected sounds into an electronic picture. What you could both see on the monitor when we were in there. So this allows us to take measurements, quite precise measurements, so we can see that the foetus is developing properly. So we pick up any obvious abnormalities. Then there's Down's Syndrome. We can measure something called nuchal translucency thickness. About 90, 91 per cent of foetuses with Down's exhibit this. No sign of it here. In this case quite normal, so the chances of your delivering a Down's baby are pretty remote. Phew, nearly gave away the sex just then. Natural to say Down's Syndrome "girl" or Down's "boy" once you know. I'll try to watch it. Anyway, as I say, we've done the sums and they all stack up properly.'

He shook hands with them both across the desk, then showed them out into the corridor and gave them directions. 'Bloody easy to get lost here. Sharp left at the water filter.'

They had gone only a few yards when he called them back.

'I should have asked but it seemed so straightforward. Any

61

questions you'd, either of you, like to ask?'

They beamed and shook their heads and turned away from the figure in his dark green corduroys.

———

So.

Since the ultrasound results were normal, and since Francesca at 27 wasn't in a high-risk group for possible birth defects, and since amniocentesis was an invasive procedure and carried a significant risk of 'disturbing' the pregnancy and (rarely) of actually damaging the foetus, she decided, on the best available medical advice, to pass on amniocentesis.

It was the rational decision, though there was still a very slight risk of undetected birth abnormality. 'And anyway,' she continued, 'what *would* we terminate for, Hamish? We wouldn't terminate for Down's, would we? Maybe spina bifida. But they can spot that on the sonograph.'

Hamish thought. 'Not going to happen,' he said. 'Pointless thought experiment.'

In some dark, unvisited place, he disagreed with her. He would have terminated the pregnancy for Down's Syndrome. He couldn't imagine the designer in Francesca faced with the imperfections caused by an extra chromosome.

(He didn't know his wife. He *couldn't* know his wife. At that stage, she didn't know herself either.)

———

'My belly button's inside out.'

A pale scar. A child's crude representation of a star. Clumsily twinkling.

They consulted their list of names and settled on Edward or Annunciata.

———

The baby girl was perfectly normal.

Birth weight 7 lbs, 3 ozs. With gluey eye, several whiteheads over her nose, cramped simian features, sucking blisters. When asleep, pink as cooked ham, red as a scald when hungry. Adorable.

And known immediately as Annie. 'There's something Scottish in that red hair. Where did *that* come from?'

She snuffled like a hedgehog when feeding from her mother's modest breasts.

———

After a day and a half two doctors, a male and a female,

called Hamish into an office just before he entered the ward. 'Could we have a word?'

'We've run some tests, routine stuff, Mr McCrae, and we're a bit concerned about your baby. You see, there are about fifteen indicators of Down's Syndrome and your baby Annunciata has five we can detect. It's not always straightforward to identify. She looked quite normal when she was born. It's not even certain now, but it's looking increasingly likely.' The man's voice was a low Yorkshire baritone.

'What are the indicators?' Hamish was surprised he could speak.

'We might hear a heart murmur. We didn't actually. Or see what are called Brushfield spots in the baby's irises. We didn't see them either. But quite a lot of things – none of them restricted to Down's babies.'

'Like what?'

'Straight, very fine hair. Low-set ears. Unusual creases on the foot-soles. A narrow, high palate. A larger than usual space between the big toe and the second toe. So you see: all possible occurrences in a normal baby. It is a question of accumulation.'

'And you found all those?'

The woman doctor took over. 'No, the palate seems normal. But we did find a simian crease in the palm. Most palms have two lateral creases. Down's Syndrome children have one. That's a serious indicator.'

'Whereas fine straight hair …'

'Exactly,' the woman doctor said. 'Or a slightly flattened back of the head. Same thing. But the simian crease taken together with the clinodactyly. That's …'

'More significant?'

'Yes'. They answered together, like a couple.

Hamish couldn't bear to look at their faces, at their concern. He looked up at the corner of the ceiling. 'What's a clino whatever it was?'

'Clinodactyly. Short curved little fingers with a single flexion furrow.'

'You're really saying it's a certainty, aren't you?'

'We're afraid so,' the Yorkshire man said.

'I'll tell my wife,' Hamish said. 'But you need to say it all again, so I can make some notes. It'll be better if I know what I'm talking about. You don't have to speak that slowly. I'm a reporter. I had to have Pitman's.'

'Pitman's?' the woman doctor asked.

'Shorthand.'

Shorthand. He could already see her waddling into the future, squat, overweight, raucous, unintelligible, wearing two hearing aids and squinting at the world through National Health specs. With short hands.

Francesca was sitting in bed, using her mobile phone to film Annie asleep in her little plastic box, tight in the sheet, but she lifted a hand in his direction by way of greeting.

Hamish laid a hand on her shoulder. 'Brace yourself, Botswana.'

'Something bad?' She didn't look round.

'The baby's Down's Syndrome.'

Francesca turned and registered the look on Hamish's face. 'I thought, I just thought, I don't know why. Something. They spent a lot of time. A lot of time.'

'I'll tell you exactly what they told me. I took notes.'

Francesca felt for his hand. 'Poor you. Poor Hamish.'

He improvised from his shorthand notes, in a low voice, expanding here and there. She listened, head bent, looking at the blue unforgettable hospital blanket – the blanket stitch, the surface texture a thick woven dust.

When Hamish finished, she looked up and met his gaze. His eyes gave away nothing, so she knew he was suffering somewhere. She knew him well enough to discount the apparent control. He was hiding his hurt from her.

'Hamish? Hamish, I love this baby.'

He squeezed her hand and said nothing.

'We talked about this. Remember you said we wouldn't terminate for Down's and I agreed. You remember that? Well, that's where we are. That's all. It isn't ideal. Of course it isn't. But I refuse to be devastated. We will deal with this. We will.'

Francesca knew very well that it had been her assertion, not Hamish's. His position on Down's was reserved, as it were. But now she needed him on her team.

———

At the fifth-floor offices of the *Sunday Times* and at the Bung Hole, their colleagues were alive to the irony – such a strikingly beautiful couple – but reluctant to broach it. They were journalists, however, so they did, as journalists do.

On 28 May 2007 the BBC journalist Laura Trevelyan was writing after the death of the journalist Vincent Hanna. She quoted a Hanna *obiter dictum*: 'simplify and then exaggerate – that's the gold rule of TV journalism.'

Not just TV journalism. A story in journalism is dramatic, backlit, eye-catching, characterised by chiaroscuro. The most beautiful couple in the world have a hideous handicapped child – and our hearts go out to them.

Bringing up Annie was more like the making of a work of art: an act of concentration, belief, craft, correction, adjustment, inspiration, candour, cunning, love of perfection and the loss of self.

———————

All artists know that they have strengths and weaknesses they can do nothing about. As Auden says, in his 'Anthem for St Cecilia's Day': 'I shall never be different. / Love me.' The artist works with what he has got, with what he has been given.

And he learns to conceal the weaknesses he cannot improve.

Thirty years ago Rudolf Nureyev appeared on *Parkinson*. The chat-show host did his best to oil his way up Nureyev's trousers in order to rim the star's star: 'What is it like to be the greatest dancer, the most perfect dancer, in the world?' Nureyev: 'It is not true. I have a fault. A tiny, tiny fault.' Parkinson: 'Tell us what it is, Rudi.'

Nureyev: 'I will not tell you.'

Francesca set to work with what she had been given.

Annunciata Williams-McCrae.

Annie.

Who was slow to make up her birth weight.

––––––––

Nearly always, Down's Syndrome comes accessorised with other disabilities. There are often heart problems, or reflux problems (violent vomiting), that require corrective surgery. Annie had neither.

Common too are difficulties with hearing, breathing and seeing. Talking is frequently a problem because of the larger tongue in the small mouth. Francesca and Annie will come to these, but first they encountered unexpected obstacles.

Down's babies come deprived of certain reflex instincts. They have to be taught. It isn't natural to them to go down stairs backwards or to brush away something covering their faces. Francesca realised that ordinary children could manage the equivalent of a sonnet sequence of actions. Whereas Annie had to be taught – again and again and again – that a rhyme was a word that sounded the same, though it wasn't the same. Francesca put a handkerchief over her face and brushed it off – pooh! Francesca put a handkerchief over Annie's face …

It was like being trapped forever in the present tense of the first line of a first reader.

Gradually it changed into a game mother and daughter played together.

How do we learn difficult things that later become automatic? There is a hard-wired instinct for learning to grip with the opposing thumb and index finger. But all children have to practise this motor skill. Down's babies have to practise more. They have to practise, patiently, like virtuoso pianists and fiddle players. You do something difficult, again and again, until it is easy. Easier.

When it comes to learning to ride a bicycle, all children are Down's for a time. The Down's children are Down's for longer, that's all. Annie Williams-McCrae learned to ride her Palm Beach roadster, first of all with stabilisers and finally without. Francesca cried with exhaustion. But the exultation … she couldn't stop laughing.

When Annie needed spectacles, Francesca made sure she had Polaris rimless lightweight glasses from Sweden. Her hearing aids were the tiniest cochlear implants – 'A condition of complete simplicity / (Costing not less than everything)', Hamish intoned as he wrote out the cheque for £7,000 (equipment and consultancy). Annie's intensive speech therapy didn't come cheaply either, but the journos at the comic started a fund. ('It's thalidomide all over again: Harry Evans thou art mighty yet.')

When the time came, orthodontistry. 'If ordinary kids can have a fucking fortune spent on fixing their teeth, why not Annie?'

'If dancers can learn, Down's can learn. It's about degrees of difficulty.' She had dancing lessons and cried and came to love music. She also loved the leg-warmers, the angora wraparounds, the silk head-scarves. She hated her gracelessness, the misery between the music and her movements. She begged Francesca to mitigate the fierce unrelenting love that insisted on the lessons. She begged by lying on the floor and screaming. Francesca sometimes said the Down's myth of sunny, mindless pliability was bullshit. But actually Annie's temperament was as equable as her parents' – and as determined, in its way. Down's children take after their parents.

She became less clumsy, achieved an awkward, determined elegance.

She was helped by Francesca's (disguised) tyrannical focus on food – only the right food in the right quantities. All three of them ate the same food, observed the same regime. No one – not Hamish, not Francesca, not Annie – was allowed to get fat. They competed on the exercise bike, but actually it was impossible to get fat. Francesca designed the menu – and it worked.

Hamish's inappropriate joke: if you don't want to be a vegetable, eat your vegetables. Vegetables. Vegetables. Vegetables. The Autobiography of Gertrude Stein.

––––––

There were other schools of thought, even among subscribers to the Beano and Dandy Fund (a reference to the comic and usually abbreviated to the B & D). 'What's wrong with accepting Down's? Isn't there something conformist, Fascist, here? What's wrong with difference? Why can't you embrace the Other?'

Francesca was brisk. 'Yea, let's all embrace obesity, alcoholism and crummy teeth. Let's accept our station in life. What is all this *acceptance*? Laziness. I accept nothing. I don't condemn fat people. I just think they should lose weight. Exercise. Exercise a bit of will power. Sorry, Godfrey.'

(Godfrey was notorious at the comic for claiming expenses for two lunches on the same day – with bills to prove it.)

'This regimen of yours, Fran, isn't it all about shame? Sorry.'

'No, that's OK. We have to talk. *Shame?* Why should I pretend that Annie's unnaturalness is natural? OK, it *is* natural. It just isn't normal. And just because I love her doesn't mean I have to love Down's. Where is it, somewhere in Walter Pater, where he says that Leonardo says that all improvements in arts stem from a sense of dissatisfaction? Something like that. In *The Renaissance* somewhere. Read it at Saint Martins for my fucking art history thesis. Why don't we give up on education, eh? On improvement? Why don't we accept ignorance?'

'Some of us fucking have!'

Hamish splashed out the wine. He and Francesca drank

Evian. Always. The banished Zippo stood exiled on the high windowsill, wearing a thin toupee of dust.

———

In varying degrees, all Down's Syndrome children have learning disabilities. From the very beginning, to improve her intelligence, Annie was given folinic acid and antioxidant vitamin supplementation (selenium 10 mcg, zinc 5 mg, vitamin A 0.9 mg, vitamin E 100 mg, vitamin C 50 mg) daily.

In a compartmentalised plastic box, a seven-day pattern of pills, an arrangement of ampoules, like a Damien Hirst.

Francesca had done all the reading, all the googling. She had read the Logan report on a randomised trial, using supplements and placebos – and its negative outcome. But she distrusted the measurement methodology – the Griffiths Developmental Quotient and the MacArthur Communicative Development Inventory (slightly adapted). What was wrong with intelligent observation?

Yes, you could kid yourself.

But you could also kid yourself with science. You could kid yourself it is 'scientific'.

Look at the methods for measuring normal intelligence. How reliable are they? What about the idiot-savant, what about the stupid genius, what about that computer hacker with Asperger's? All those dyslexics: Richard Rogers probably couldn't spell architecture. The ruler, the method of measurement, comes with implicit assumptions. Think of the second-class Oxford degrees handed down to Matthew Arnold and Arthur Hugh Clough. Think of all the thirds awarded at Oxford by professional assessors – to Auden, Betjeman, Evelyn Waugh. Think of all those people with first-class degrees forever stupid with conceit. You can't measure poetry. How do you measure a 'childish', 'naive' drawing by Constantin Brancusi?

––––––––

Which brings us to beauty and what it is.

'I want to re-brand Down's,' Francesca said to Hamish over the lid of her lap-top. 'What is wrong with Mongol? It's brilliant. It's accurate and it *isn't* insulting. The Mongols were a beautiful race of warriors. Come and look at this.'

She showed him the home page of the website of the British Down's Syndrome Association. At the top there was a window where the faces of Down's children came and went. 'It's a budget Bill Viola, I know. But, Hamish, look. She's beautiful. And so is that black girl. They *are.* OK, *he* isn't. But look at *him.*'

'It's a clever and biased selection,' Hamish said. 'It's feel-good, is what it is.'

'I know that,' she said impatiently. 'But the point, the point is some Down's *are* beautiful. Not all of them, any more than all normal people are beautiful. It's always a proportion. But these kids here, most of them, are indisputably beautiful.' She gestured at the screen.

'So?' Hamish looked at her with his navy-blue eyes.

'Black is beautiful. Redesign beauty. Not "the repulsive mask of a nigger's soul". [Conrad was a reference point for both] Angela Davis. Don't straighten your hair.'

Hamish burst out laughing. 'Oh that *is* rich, Botswana.'

Although Annie's hair was less thin and straight, less sparse than originally seemed likely, Francesca had strengthened it by regularly shaving it off. 'Think hairs on your legs. Think how a boy's bum-fluff responds to the razor.'

It reminded Hamish a bit of Britten's hair. Francesca preferred to think of Emily Dickinson's chestnut burr. It had definitely thickened, but neither comparison was correct. It was softer than either suggests. And it was a gold-red of real allure.

———

I think she was right.

The Down's face can be very beautiful.

Let me describe the face of Annunciata Williams-McCrae at the age of 16.

Begin with the soft smelted upturned heart-shaped mouth made for smiling a smile kept for kindness, tenderness, incapable of malice.

Am I going too fast for you?

But the face is streamlined. Neither clipped nor curt. An aerodynamic design.

The almond eyes see out through their sleepy epicanthic fold. Trusting and calm, if a flicker from slowness, a further flicker from stupidity.

Settled in slow-motion beauty, heart-breaking beauty.

PART IV

Heart Failure

Enobarbus

In the classic ghost story, there is always a sceptic who is gradually persuaded. This character is a reader surrogate raising objections on our behalf – and quelling them.

Enobarbus is our shrewd representative, our level-headed, even cynical, delegate at the court of Queen Cleopatra. First, he is a laconic professional soldier, a man of few words in an Egyptian retinue of motormouths and babblers. Prose is his first medium. Antony tells Enobarbus that Fulvia (his estranged wife) is dead and Enobarbus tells it how it is: basically a blessing; a woman who can now be replaced by another, whereas formerly she was displaced. It is noteworthy that he frames the situation generically – one smock replaced by another petticoat, rather than Fulvia and Cleopatra.

No allowance for individuals.

We have already witnessed Antony soliloquising regretfully, plausibly, about the dead Fulvia: 'the hand could pluck her back that shoved her on.' His feelings are convincingly mixed.

Enobarbus is – how can I put this? – waterproof. That is his character note.

And yet he is given the great speech of tribute to Cleopatra: 'The barge she sat in …' What does this speech, virtually straight from Plutarch, tell us? Because it issues from Enobarbus – a third cousin twice removed of 'honest' Iago, 'plain' Iago – we credit its hyperbole. We know he is resistant to sentiment.

It is this resistance to emotion, his mistrust of exaggeration, of romantic distortion, that makes him modernist, a classicist before his time.

When he decides to desert Antony, he has two reasons. Antony looks like a loser, of course. But *how* he is losing is more important to Enobarbus than the defeats themselves. At Actium, instead of fighting on after Cleopatra's ships took flight, Antony follows his heart instead of his head – and deserts his navy.

Then Antony rejects Caesar's ultimatum and instead challenges Caesar to single combat. Caesar finds this laughable ('meantime / Laugh at his challenge'). For Enobarbus, the personal challenge to hand-to-hand combat is a kind of cognitive dissonance in Antony. His external circumstances – defeat and the real possibility of long-term failure – are distorting his judgement, his assessment of the situation.

The scene with the servants follows. Surrounded by his summoned 'sad captains', Antony thanks them for their loyalty, wishes he were multiple and they singular, so that he might serve them. He is rather like those actors who refuse to take a bow but instead applaud the audience. (For what?

To say 'thank you' for coming and paying attention. But this misunderstands the nature of applause – which isn't to thank the actors but to applaud them, to praise them for a demonstration of the actor's art. Applause is an act of criticism.)

At the feast, Antony is imagining his failure and indulging in self-pity. 'CLEOPATRA [*aside to Enobarbus*]: What does he mean? ENOBARBUS [*aside to Cleopatra*]: To make his followers weep'. Enobarbus despises it but cannot help responding: 'And I, an ass, am onion-eyed. For shame! | Transform us not to women!' This is the second time that Enobarbus has invoked the onion. The first was when Fulvia's death was announced by Antony: 'indeed the tears live in an onion that should water this sorrow.' At the feast Antony wants his audience to feel sorry for him by envisaging the scenario of failure. He is indulging his sentimentality, and Enobarbus is moved and revolted.

It is this unlikely character, the vigilant, emotionally sceptical Enobarbus, whom Shakespeare chooses to illustrate his thesis: that it is possible to die of a broken heart, that *More* Die *of Heartbreak*, the title of Saul Bellow's 1987 novel (my roman). Here is a character whose emotional susceptibility is suspect to himself. 'And I, an ass, am onion-eyed.' He is a hard case.

Enobarbus is mentioned only passingly in Plutarch, so is essentially Shakespeare's own invention, created for a double Shakespearean purpose: to complicate our ideas of betrayal and to test the idea of heartbreak to actual destruction.

When he has switched sides, Enobarbus hears Caesar ordering that deserters from Antony should be put in the front of the battle. He remembers how poorly rewarded Alexas was – hanged – for persuading Herod to side with Caesar instead of Antony. He has joined the apparatchiks at the opposite end of the spectrum from romantic Antony.

The romantic Antony, who, on hearing Enobarbus has deserted, blames himself and sends his chests and treasure after him with 'gentle adieus and greetings'. Antony is blind, oblivious to the injury. He can only blame himself if such an 'honest' man has gone over to the other side.

It is this act of selfless generosity that breaks Enobarbus's heart. 'This blows my heart.' What does that verb 'blows' signify? I don't think it is a converted noun from a blow. It doesn't mean 'This strikes my heart'. The image is rather that of an egg, mere shell and sudden frailty, effective as of now, now the substance is gone – blown. Shakespeare is interested in converting an emotional state into a physical state – heartbreak into heart failure. The speech continues: 'If swift thought break it not, a swifter mean / Shall out-strike thought; but thought will do't, I feel.' Let me paraphrase: the thought of my treachery and Antony's generosity will break my heart. If that thought doesn't break my heart, there is a swifter means – suicide. However, Enobarbus thinks thought will be enough.

The staging of this crucial moment is a rare Shakespearean failure. Enobarbus indicts himself in undistinguished verse and has to be overheard by curious soldiers so that his body can be removed at the scene's end and the stage cleared. We, the audience, are uncertain if Enobarbus has chosen the Roman way of suicide or not. We don't see a weapon and the soldiers report that he seems asleep. It is they who have to tell us Enobarbus is dead – because dying of heartbreak, unlike dying of a heart attack, is difficult to stage. And then the soldiers have to tell us he may still be alive and revivable. Were he dead, they would simply leave his body where it lay – inconveniently for the next scene.

Near the beginning of this scene, Enobarbus reverts to his heart condition: 'Throw my heart | Against the flint and hardness of my fault, | Which, being dried with grief, will break to powder …' Heartbreak isn't an easy thing to write about: breakage depends on the thing being brittle, and the translation of the emotional into the physical is almost mandatory. Once you address the subject of heartbreak, you address the invisible metaphor that gives the word its force.

(When William Einhorn arranges for Augie to lose his virginity with a whore in *The Adventures of Augie March*, Augie finally encounters 'the imposing female fact, the brilliant, profound thing'. The great, unexpected adjective here is 'brilliant'. In other words, Augie thinks that the female sexual organ is a *great idea*. This value judgement is transferred, unequivocally, to the vagina, which becomes 'brilliant', as if the vagina had had the thought itself. The sexual becomes intellectual in an incomparable sleight of hand.

Just as heartbreak, in Shakespeare, becomes heart failure, when the topos of heartbreak is re-written. Typically, at the same time, Shakespeare also re-writes the topos of betrayal. Like the pianist Glenn Gould learning a piece while listening to another.)

All That Flesh and Blood

In head-phones, Evgeny Karnizis was celebrating his 85th birthday alone with a new CD of Mozart's only surviving bassoon concerto.

Two others have simply disappeared, with a trace. (Obviously, or we wouldn't know about them.)

The Bassoon Concerto in B Flat, K. 191, is an intricate piece, testing for the performer, and Evgeny was listening not only to Mozart's musical invention but also to the closely miked bassoonist taking her breaths. Quick breaths. Bigger, less audible breaths. Before runs. In the middle of runs. In surprising places – to a non-performer. The player knows what is coming up and what breath will be needed to execute the next passage.

The player is in the hereafter as well as the here and now.

The listener, though, unless he knows the music well – and who knows Mozart's bassoon concerto well? – is continually surprised by what comes next. He wouldn't know where to breathe. As it happens, he was in any case holding his breath at the 18-year-old composer's brilliance. He breathed when he had to.

When he heard the breaths taken, Evgeny experienced a thrill which surprised him. Why? He didn't know why. Viscerally, he was reminded of those great arias of sexual excitement that issue from such crude physical premises – those tight, trembling reeds, those loose, rattling reeds, those split reeds, those biblical broken reeds.

All this unreliable flesh and blood and breath on which ecstasy depends.

Heaven and earth.

Just at that moment, at his kitchen table, the crown on Evgeny's right-front tooth broke off.

He wasn't eating crusty bread, or a turgid caramel, or an amber strip of pork crackling, the caked, waxy, molten crumbs. He was simply listening to Mozart's bassoon concerto in the peace of his flat in Piraeus. His wife was recovering – *Gott sei Dank* – from her radical mastectomy in Berlin. He was nursing his faulty heart away from the turmoil – to his daughter's uncontained indignation. 'You cowardly hypochondriac.'

He peered into the shaving mirror in his cramped, dank, windowless bathroom and opened his mouth like a threatened baboon. It was the side of the mirror that magnified. As he bared his teeth, he looked, he thought, like an ugly, unhappy, cowardly hypochondriac.

The crown was the work of his expensive private dentist in Kantstrasse. He put it for safe-keeping in a compartment of his medication dispenser, a maze of *de facto* colour-coded concentrations. A hive of cluster-pills, daily lozenges, bipartite grubs.

———

It was a September morning, two months later. Evgeny had just lit a cork-tipped cigarette, the first of the day, and wedged it in the rampart of the ash-tray, when he experienced acute dyspepsia that quickened, concentrated into a filament of fire. He found it hard to breathe. There seemed no room for his lungs in the great heat that was crowding his thorax. He thought he might burst into flames.

He scrabbled the pill organiser towards him and felt blindly for the *Infarkt* ampoule which would relieve this constriction that was crushing him like a boa constrictor.

He fumbled among the medication and swallowed the crown from his right-front tooth with some difficulty.

In the Metaxa ash-tray, taken from the taverna down his street, the cigarette laid its unbroken ashy spectre.

Outside, agitated, restless, Piraeus harbour worked like mercury in the morning sun. Its dark silvers reflected nothing.

PART V

Desert Island Discs

As the Actress Said to the Bishop

There were only seven years between them. She was 16. Mr Bishop was 23 or 24. But Milly thought of her English teacher as an old man – someone like her parents.

She was insolent in her bearing. It was the way she held her head to the side, her cocked gaze and the sceptical eyes. She could place her long hands akimbo at her waist in a way that seemed to weigh you and find you wanting. She didn't smile much. The teachers didn't like her and the mention of her name would solicit a common-room chorus from George Formby: 'A'm leaning on a lamp-post / At the corner of the street.' Milly was very tall. She had a long upper lip – a pinny to the other girls' aprons – and a compressed ironical mouth. She wasn't pretty but she could make people look at her. She said hardly anything, yet everyone knew who she was.

It was stage presence. As Mr Bishop realised. She exercised her power to make people look without knowing what it was she was doing. It looked like insolence but it was only the power to command the eyes. And of course it seemed like showing off, but she wasn't doing anything. She was attractive without being attractive. Flat-chested, without a waist, with no discernible buttocks, she was as innocent as an electromagnet. And her accent was south of the river.

Mr Bishop got them to read some Shakespeare in a double period. Milly read Goneril, her glottal stops ('li'ul'), her 'somefinks', evident but made crisp with consonants in private conversation, murmurous with insincerity in public. So, not overplayed hypocrisy, rather a little rushed, as if shy to show her feeling for her father. Shakespeare's words for Goneril's gross flattery but with their delivery muted – awed by the ceremonial occasion. And when she talked with Regan (Polly Evans: the cleverest in the class and disappointed not to be Cordelia), Milly let you sense her impatience to interrupt, as if her sister were a little slow. As if Goneril were the elder. Which she is. Milly had made something of Shakespeare's careless fact. You couldn't call it a hint. It wasn't a clue to the character, set up by Shakespeare. It was made into a clue by Milly, by the actress – already aware that you can't play a single characteristic, the one note, here, duplicity. You need notes to make music on stage, so the creation can sing.

Mr Bishop wondered if anyone else had noticed. The class had noticed, without noticing. They looked at Milly differently, as if they had discovered she could do something surprising, like walk on her hands.

And Milly had noticed. 'We need more time, sir, to think about how we say it. I don't mean the words, though you have to know what they mean. I mean, what's behind them. Know what I mean?'

Many Happy Returns

In *The Spoils of Poynton*, with only four main characters, Henry James composes a beautiful chamber piece. Adela Gereth, Owen Gereth, Fleda Vetch and Mona Brigstock. Of these four, only two are properly articulate. Mona is mute with malice. Owen is as dense as a tailor's block but a thing of beauty.

Henry James alludes obliquely to the virtuous paucity of his materials when he has his heroine discuss the maiden aunt at Ricks, who has furnished forth her modest cottage and made poetry out of two or three sticks of furniture, 'no more'. All this is in contrast to what James designates the 'great chorus' of Poynton, with its huge agglomeration of beautiful artefacts.

In his autobiography Stravinsky relates that the first music he remembers was made by a peasant, working his hand in his armpit to produce a rhythmic farting.

In her poem 'Poetry', Marianne Moore affects to disparage her own art as 'all this fiddle'. Perhaps she is, after all, sincere. She was a stringent moralist and much of poetry in the making is the fiddle with a few items. You lay a word against another and wait. You try another word. And another. Yet another. You wait. You begin again. Listening. Looking. For the elusive inevitable thing which has to arrive before it is recognised. And, like Odysseus, may not be recognised at first.

It is the most testing form of patience. It is never certain when you've got it out.

In *Areté* 24 (Winter 2007), Robert Craft remembered Stravinsky: 'Stravinsky's greatest qualities were his powers of concentration in music and his equally strong powers of patience. He could wait three or four days to be certain of a single note. In everything else, he was the most impatient man I have ever met.'

At Blackbird Pie, Andrew helps with the horses. He goes to the stables and he helps with the horses.

On his holidays, Andrew goes for walks with his father. Sometimes they go for a drive in the Subaru and Andrew plays a game. He lowers his electric window if his father has closed it. Or he puts it up if his father has wound it down. Andrew knows that his father knows, even though he talks about other things as if he hasn't noticed. Sometimes his father tells him that it is too cold to have the windows down.

Andrew likes looking through the Argos catalogue. It has a

lot of pages and on every page there are several illustrations.

Andrew sometimes plays with an elastic band. He waves it in the air.

If he is bored, Andrew belches. Or makes other noises to amuse himself.

Now and then, Andrew glances at the television. He watches television only when there is *Doctor Who*.

He has been to the *Doctor Who* exhibition with Louise. Andrew saw a Time Lord there.

Andrew likes lunch very much. And he likes tea, especially with chocolate cake. He likes Cadbury's milk-chocolate fingers.

Andrew sometimes waves an elastic band. He likes the smell.

Andrew has a girlfriend at Blackbird Pie. She kissed him in the bathroom. Andrew also loves Louise.

Andrew went on his holidays with two pairs of pyjama bottoms and no pyjama tops, instead of one pair of pyjama bottoms and one pyjama top.

Andrew's father gave him a toothbrush and three *Doctor Who* DVDs.

Andrew has a girlfriend who kissed him in the bathroom.

Andrew likes to wave an elastic band.

Andrew wears a baseball cap. Andrew hasn't much hair. Baldness is caused by the Time Destructor. This year he is 37 or 38. For his birthday, there was a chocolate cake.

Andrew's life is like a villanelle.

If he is bored, he belches. Or makes noises to amuse himself.

Andrew's life is full of strangeness that he doesn't understand. Louise looks under the bed where he doesn't look. No Daleks there, she says, and switches off his light. Andrew goes to sleep bravely.

Andrew's life is like a villanelle.

Fashion Statement

You probably think Mr Bishop was wearing pedagogical flannels and a Donegal tweed jacket with protective leather cuffs. (Donegal tweed: a blood-flecked Jackson Pollock on Ritalin.) In fact, he favoured black skinny jeans (501s), Oakleys and a black bomber jacket. ('Headmaster? Nothing about mutton dressed as lamb, as you put it, in my conditions of employment that I can recall.')

Quite cool, except that all the kids were into hoodies and baggies in a state of arrested collapse – or saggies, as Mr Bishop privately thought of them. Not that they were allowed in school. There was a uniform of military brown and greens – which the kids transformed to a slovenly chic. No one tucked in their shirt. Every tie was a catapult. Flannel trousers heaped up cubist asymmetries on their shoes. Shoelaces were undone, entailing a suicide-risk cell-block shuffle. The school blazer was worn off the shoulders. A demoralised, retreating army of ironic fashionistas, too cool to be triumphalist. Hanging loose.

No wonder Milly thought Mr Bishop was like her parents. Quite cool isn't hot. Cool is hot. This is how fashion works. By exclusion. Which is why fashion has to change. As soon as it is 'fashionable', really popular, it is by definition 'common' and therefore unfashionable. Fashion is like the avant-garde – which expects to be disliked, ridiculed, triumphant. Adverse reaction is incorporated into its aesthetic. In the arts – literature, painting – this takes time. In fashion, the process is accelerated. It is its own Large Hadron Collider. The method? Mass hypnosis – beautiful people confer their beauty on the clothes, for everyone to see, and so fashion outfaces and embraces the offensive, the ridiculous.

Milly thought Mr Bishop looked old but that didn't make any difference. She decided to fuck him anyway. She could see he was useful. So he could have the use of her in return. Her tits and her bits. Why not? They weren't important to her. Only acting was.

You Don't Understand

They were having a coffee at the Starbucks across the road from St Jude's: 'Let's lose this glazed-shit ceramic, what do you say?' Mr Bishop's impatient gesture multiplied in the glaze. He looked at her across the table – her dull red hair, her freckles, her wide nostrils and her ugly expressive mouth. 'So, you're serious, yes? You want to act? For a living, as a career?'

She held his eyes and lowered her cup so that there was nothing between him and her lips. 'No. You don't understand, sir. I don't want to be an actress. I am going to be a great actress.'

Bishop was impressed by her solemnity and also experienced an imp of laughter tickling his armpit. He looked up at the ornate plaster ceiling. 'Phew. OK. I hear you. Maybe we could make a start on the great actress project by getting on first-name terms. I'm David. Well, from now on in private. Better be "sir" still at school. But like this, Milly, David is fine.'

'OK, David.'

Milly added to herself: And you are going to help me to be a great actress and I will fuck you to make sure.

Breakfast at the Bishops'

The trouble with Milly's plan was that Bishop didn't desire her at all. His motive was altruism. He thought she could act. And that someone should save her for the stage. She didn't deserve the shelving detail at Tesco, not with her talent.

Sex?

Bishop didn't see her that way at all.

'What does she call you, the cuckoo? Does she call you David now?'

Bishop's wife was scraping butter over her toast. She stopped and imitated a cuckoo calling, 'Dav-id. Dav-id.'

He looked in the direction of the covered buttons on her quilted housecoat. (*Going up. Lingerie and Leisure Wear.*) 'Pretty good. You should be an actress.'

'Fuck right off, all right? I know you despise my job.' She was a secretary in the Arts and Humanities division of King's College. London. Every day she walked over Waterloo Bridge to the Strand.

'Barbara, I do not despise your job. What's so glitzy about teaching English and drama in a Hackney sink?'

'Perhaps it's your glinting, pathetic Oakleys. All I'm saying is watch yourself. Be careful. You'll be wanting to fuck her. (Don't do that.) I know you.'

'Do what?'

'Pull that face.' She pulled the face. 'I know you. For the highest reasons, naturally, but you'll still end up fucking her. The saintly, social deprivation fuck, the eco-friendly fuck. I know you.'

She did know him. But not as well as she thought. She was ten years older than Bishop and wary. She knew how easy it had been to get him to marry her. His one night with a policewoman at Hendon Training College, his troubled confession and her prolonged tearful outrage had been enough.

But it wasn't Barbara's anger, or his guilt, that changed his mind. He was touched that she cared, cared for him – when most of the time she behaved as if she couldn't care less. Bishop had been thinking of going off with the enthusiastic, athletic trainee WPC. His confession was intended as the prelude to a more definitive declaration. He wasn't cowed, as Barbara believed; he was helpless in the face of her hurt.

'Barbara, look, you should see the girl. Just see her. You'll see.' He shook his head and smiled. 'She's thin. I mean, everywhere. She's about as sexy as a ruler. And she isn't pretty. She's got something, but it isn't a black belt in the boudoir. Promise.'

'And I mind about the money you're wasting. Theatre isn't cheap.'

'She has to see real theatre. Previews. Cheapest seats. Standing. And I'm applying for a school bursary. Not much, but better than nothing. Try to be generous.'

———

Bishop's mind had been an empty horizon, a line, an innocent line, geometry's uninterrupted point in motion – graphite in the morning, iodine in the evening. Barbara's jealousy had him watching for a speck of interest.

Kristin Scott Thomas at the Royal Court

'She has a mannerism. Did you notice?'

They were in the Downstairs Bar, drinking tap water and, between bites, holding their home-made cheese sandwiches under the table.

'I think she's a brilliant Arkadina.'

'You just think she's beautiful. She *is* beautiful. Fantastic. Those eyelids,' Milly said. 'But she's got a tell. Like a poker player. She doesn't think she's beautiful. Or beautiful enough. You must have noticed.'

Bishop raised his eyebrows.

'The thing about being beautiful,' Milly continued, 'is that it's great while it lasts. But it doesn't last. It can't. So you start to feel anxious. Beautiful, but anxious. At first, the anxiousness looks like acting. You pass it off as acting. It gives you an expression to your beauty. An accent. So you're not just a beautiful egg like Emmanuelle Béart. But really it's just that you're afraid the audience will notice the signs. That your beauty is threatened.'

'And you saw the signs?' Bishop's question wasn't really a question.

'How many kids has she had?'

'Dunno. Two or three, I think. By that French doctor.'

'That's why she doesn't like being looked at. It isn't the face. The face is fabulous. It's her belly she doesn't like, doesn't trust. Watch her right hand. Never stops smoothing her dress over her tummy. OK. OK. Never is an exaggeration. You know what I mean.'

It was true. He checked in the second half.

Kristin Scott Thomas with stretch marks, smocking, the navel in its plump stoup.

'Thing is,' Milly added before they went their opposite directions on the tube, 'that insecurity is great for Arkadina. Trigorin fancies Nina because she's younger. Arkadina has a grown-up son.'

'So it was deliberate, you think?' Bishop asked.

'Might be. Might not be. Might have been intuitive. Or maybe she does it all the time. We'll have to see her in something else. There's my train. Bye.'

She ran for the escalator, her raincoat buoyed behind her, and skittered sideways down the steps like a foal.

————

And that was how Milly worked as an actress. She saw everything. She understood Kristin Scott Thomas as

Arkadina, and Kristin Scott Thomas as Kristin Scott Thomas. She could have played either.

Or both together.

Her Greatest Role

Except, of course, that she wasn't beautiful. Nor was she sexually attractive.

And both these deficiencies were a problem for Milly's plan to seduce Bishop and permanently lock his investment in her futures.

Bishop and she drove to a Stratford matinee, where they saw Harriet Walter as Cleopatra, opposite Patrick Stewart as Antony. Obviously but undetectably, Walter shop-lifted the show. Even the vigilant, fault-finding Milly had to concede her greatness.

Harriet Walter's face is versatile rather than striking or beautiful. In Martha Fiennes's film *Chromophobia* she played a judge's wife, dead-heading roses, grubbing in the flower beds, removing moss with a broken kitchen knife in her big hand. There was an element of knuckle in her irregular nose. Her lips were thin, her jaw a handful for those big hands. A judge's wife, in fact: loyal, long-suffering, bony, lean-faced, asexual, a little bit mannish.

In *Antony and Cleopatra* she was beautiful, confident, sexy. It was a lesson for Milly, but a lesson she wasn't quite sure she'd understood. She could see the result, but she needed to study the working. Was Harriet Walter unequivocally beautiful? Obviously not. You only had to look. But she was *equivocally* beautiful.

How was it done? It was largely the confident, quietly virtuosic voice. Saying Shakespeare's lines. In opera, great music can transfigure mediocre words. Here it seemed the reverse: great words, expressively delivered, performed their plastic surgery. Creating not a young woman complacently voluptuous on the sun-bed of her own aura, but a beautiful, knowing, older woman, confident of her powers.

She was the opposite of Kristin Scott Thomas in her unwavering self-belief.

Her Cleopatra had no tell. She looked like a woman who liked being looked at. She was fit – trained up to it, unfaltering.

From Harriet Walter, Milly learned that self-belief is something you can act.

She auditioned for the difficult part of irresistible woman. She prepared by starting with the voice. Bishop had persuaded Hilda Sams, a voice coach at the National, to take on Milly for free.

'What we do is, we expand your natural range. Just a bit. We don't fundamentally change the middle of your voice. We don't want you to sound like an ac-*tor*.'

'What about my accent? That's in the mid'lle of my voice. My glot'll stop.'

'Easy. First, what I'm going to do is make you American. East Coast Boston. Can you hear that "o" in Boston? Rhymes with Jane Austen. Sort of.'

Milly wondered aloud why they were starting on advanced voice coaching. 'Shouldn't I learn to speak English first?'

'Seems illogical, I know. But I want to teach you something fundamental about the way we speak. OK if I smoke?' Hilda was a fat woman in dungarees with Doc Martens. Milly was already making mental notes on how she made a cigarette.

'What it is, is, to imitate a sound, you need to imitate the face, to reconfigure your mouth, actually your entire body language. That's how the best impersonators work. Look at Rory Bremner. First of all, he makes himself look like Tony Blair and the voice comes from the feel of being in Blair's body. The look isn't an optional extra to make the voice more convincing. The look unlocks the voice.'

'You speak better French if you try to look Franch?' Gamine Milly pouted for Hilda and brought her hands into play.

'Crudely, yes. You don't learn an accent unless you learn how the voice looks in action, how it feels. Meryl Streep, Gwyneth Paltrow, have both done perfect English accents.

If you asked them: now, do a fucking English accent now, they couldn't. They wouldn't. They'd have to relearn how that voice is made.'

'So,' Milly asked, 'is it that the body affects the voice?'

'The mouth, the whole head, everything.'

'But it's gonna be a two-way street,' Milly urged. 'The voice also affects the body. Surely?'

Hilda blew searchlights of smoke. 'David said you were quick. You are.'

They started on a few phrases of East Coast American. First in English and then in American, so Milly could feel the difference in her mouth. Then in American. Then in American.

'*I can see no way out but through – leastways for me – and then they'll be convinced.*'

'*Pal, you have too many irons in the fire.*'

Milly was wondering whether she should fuck Hilda and what transferable skills she would learn if she did. She could rehearse being irresistible with her.

———

Sexually, Milly had no skills. Or no skills she knew about.

(For example, Hilda wasn't a lesbian. The Doc Martens and

the dungarees were theatre Doc Martens and dungarees. They said you worked in the engine room and not in the spotlight, back stage rather than out on the boards. Interesting too what 'fat' signifies in the context of Doc Martens and dungarees. If Hilda had been 'thin', she might have read as heterosexual, despite the dungarees. 'Fat': there is a prejudice here that lesbians are lesbians *faute de mieux*, unable to attract the opposite sex.)

How was Milly to acquire the necessary sexual skills? How do we acquire sexual skills? Are they strictly inherent? – something implied by the alternative phrase, *sexually gifted*. (Or not.)

Musically gifted. Poetically gifted. These epithets imply an unassailable advantage – like Grace in religion – conferred from outside or above. But consider the phrase 'athletically gifted' and the connotation of 'gifted' is modified. The gifted person has an initial advantage that requires work, application, enhancement, improvement. Talent is a combination of talent and application.

Only in the context of the arts is this unclear – thanks to the sentimental concept of genius. The myth of Philoctetes – the wound and the bow – predicates genius on disability. Is genius the result of external factors? – upbringing, suffering, patriarchal tyranny, claustrophobic mothering? Obviously not: there are thousands of suffering, oppressed, over-protected, filially crushed individuals who never look like turning into Kafka, or the caricature that passes for

Kafka in literary studies. No one applies this absurd idea to cricket players, for example. Was Don Bradman a great batsman because he was orphaned at the age of eight (not that he was)?

What are sexual gifts anyway? *She was a genius in bed.* What does this mean? It isn't quite the absolute the word implies. For instance, a sexually gifted wife may cease to be a sexually gifted wife with her husband – because she has taken a lover, on whom she now showers her gifts; or because the husband has taken a lover and becomes less interested in calling forth her sexual gifts. There is a truth here somewhere. I think it is this. Not that man is naturally monogamous – rather that the sexual appetite is limited, not boundless. The gifts are not inexhaustible.

Sexual gifts are actually singular – the gift of enjoyment of what is there, however many forms this may take. Distaste is fatal in this notoriously tasteless area, which is full of acquired tastes. (The taste of semen, the taste of vagina, the differing tastes of both.) Yet it is possible to enjoy distaste itself if it is incorporated, made a part of desire. The sexually gifted also know that although sex can be an expression of love, it isn't intrinsically personalised – that sexual excitement, that sexual incitement, is self-centred, blamelessly self-centred. And of course self-censorship is as fatal as distaste. Oscar Wilde spoke of the love that dare not speak its name. Repression, the refusal of authentic desire, prescription and proscription (P & P), are worse if they are DIY. For the sexually gifted, 'the love that dare not speak its name' speaks and names its unspeakable desires.

We are happy with Cleopatra: 'a lover's pinch, / That hurts and is desired.' That isn't a synecdoche for widespread, viral S & M, it is hallowed literature. We are less happy with spanking – which is a source of reliable comedy, as Paul Johnson has discovered. Ken Tynan, another spankee, has been treated with less ribaldry. Because he has literary credentials. If you substitute 'smack' for 'spank', the activity loses a bit of its comedy. (Some, of course, will see comedy as an essential part of the exciting humiliation which spanking represents.) I should say that the desire to smack flesh is more common than is usually admitted, though not universal.

In 'Wife-Wooing', Updike claims kin with James Joyce: 'There is a line of Joyce. I try to recover it from the legendary, imperfectly explored grottoes of *Ulysses*: a garter snapped, to please Blazes Boylan, in a deep Dublin den. What? Smackwarm. That was the crucial word. Smacked smackwarm on her smackable warm woman's thigh.' In Ian McEwan's *The Innocent*, Leonard, the hero, gradually persuades himself that his sexual partner Maria would like to be smacked. She doesn't. Her previous relationship was physically abusive.

Not everything can be shared, but nothing should be denied. Many marriages exist in denial, squandering these precious, sordid gifts. The gifted revel in these gifts – privately, guiltily, without a qualm. We have to accept our desires with gratitude. The worst condition, set down in Ecclesiastes, is 'when desire shall fail'.

Milly, of course, was up for anything. In principle.

But she needed to know what it was she was excited by – which, of course, would change.

She searched and researched her mind for what was there. Nothing was missing. She just had to look long enough. Regan. Goneril. Cordelia. Cruelty and tenderness. Degradation. Sentiment.

———

Milly had never masturbated. But when she started, she recalled the sensation of soap at bath-time. Not a vivid recall, an exact recall. *That.* Nice enough but nothing special. *This* was sex? An unfocused aura of well-being, of pleasant sensation, but nothing acute, nothing imperative. A wash of background music on the edge of inaudibility. But then she thought of strings buzzing and a fly entered her mind, grooming its hairy legs and glistening wings – a gross, wrinkled, restless fly searching for something dirty to settle on, something improper, something forbidden. She knew she shouldn't be thinking these things. And she crawled with intricate excitement.

She had discovered the aphrodisiac of guilt.

Quickly, what was ludicrous or unlikely or obscene or

grubby attracted her interest once her distaste was diminished. The perverse came naturally to Milly. There was what made her wet and what, after a longish interregnum, actually made her come. Mild interest overtaken by obscenity.

Mind over matter.

Though matter inspired mind.

Hilda was right. Everything was two-way traffic.

———————

There is a mythical story about Laurence Olivier and Dustin Hoffman, who co-starred in *Marathon Man*. At some stage of the filming the plot required Hoffman to be exhausted from sleeplessness. So Hoffman stayed awake for three nights until he was exhausted – and ready for filming. Olivier is reputed to have asked, 'Have you ever thought of acting?'

There is a profound misunderstanding in this malicious anecdote about the nature of acting. A false opposition of technique (faking it) and method (living it), of trained Olivier versus literalist Hoffman. Acting is like literature in this respect. We read a book. We cry over the fate of its characters. We know the characters are not real. This is the theme of Tom Stoppard's *Rosencrantz and Guildenstern Are Dead*: their fate is assigned by Stoppard's title and Shakespeare's antecedent play. They are fictions without back stories, they are without free will. Yet they have the illusion of free will – illustrated by the boat that takes them to England and their deaths. On the boat, they are free to walk around, to choose their movements, direct their actions – but they cannot alter the course of the boat or their destiny. Guildenstern reflects that the nails grow after death – an emblem of their situation. When they look for their pasts, they discover they are effectively non-existent. Is Hamlet their friend? Guildenstern tells Rosencrantz: 'You have only their word for it.' They are not real people. They are functions of the drama as well as functionaries within it. They only feel real to themselves and to us – the audience who knows they are not real, but pities them anyway.

An actor in performance is in the moment on stage and also aware of the person in Row C who is drinking from a polystyrene cup – as Ralph Fiennes revealed in *Areté* 3 (Autumn 2000). Human beings are capable of living in contradiction, of thinking two opposite equally truthful things at once. The actor pretends. The actor's pretence is authentic – just as all art is sincere and artifice.

Hoffman and Olivier share a common aim: a character that reads as unquestionably true. Both actors are immersed in the moment when they perform and outside themselves monitoring the quality control. There is no opposition between 'technique' and method acting. Method acting is another technique – another technique serving the same end.

To her voice training with Hilda, Milly added the method, prolonged immersion in her chosen part. She was never out of character. Not a seductress. Not a caricature of sexuality, sustained on the wing-beat of her false eyelashes. Only someone seductive, someone desirable, someone potentially addictive.

And Milly discovered that true seduction wasn't about display. Desirable women were desired, all the time, by undesirable men, so they concealed their gifts. They affected to be unaware of their desirability. They wore the dark goose-flesh of their cleavage matter-of-factly. Seductive women kept acknowledgement out of their neutral tantalising eyes.

Because they had it, they hid it.

They created a vacuum – and, with it, the promise of plenitude, the mirage of wetness.

All you had to create was thirst.

Which you did by being a desert.

But a desert whose sand was sometimes inexplicably pitted with rain, whose pitted rock was suddenly darkened, whose dust was darkly laid. All you needed was a lizard, like a tic douloureux. Like a tell in poker.

———

Bishop thought Milly was definitely different, in some

indefinable way. She had something he couldn't quite see. It was there – until you looked.

He began to watch her closely, surreptitiously, as you look at a beautiful woman.

And Then He Kissed Me

When at last he tried to kiss her, she turned away – with parted, ready lips.

'I think I should save you from yourself. Think about Barbara. I wouldn't want to harm your marriage.'

Something Milly had prepared beforehand. The perfect starter. Consideration on a bed of fresh qualms.

On the floor, another educated choice. As he entered her, Bishop met the mild resistance of her hymen. He saw her hide the shadow on her face – and smile uncertainly. He was touched and aroused.

'You're a virgin.'

She nodded. 'You'll have to teach me everything. Everything you want me to do. Anything.'

Her hymen gave and Bishop was instantly overpowered by his orgasm.

It had taken less than five minutes from beginning to end.

She kissed him. Then she kissed his half-cocked cock.

'I don't think we should ever do this again,' she said. 'You could lose your job.'

It was her final inspiration.

—————

Soon they were fucking as much as was compatible with unremitting focus on her acting.

RADA

Milly auditioned for a place at RADA. They prepared the two passages for audition – chosen to show her emotional range – Sasha's speech about love in *Ivanov* and (daringly) Iago's 'And what's he, then, that says I play the villain?' On the one hand, Sasha's naive, impractical endorsement of love as full-time female servitude: 'But love is our whole existence! I love you, and that means I long to cure your unhappiness and go with you to the ends of the earth.' On the other hand, Iago's cynical improvisation of a plan.

So, a contrast.

But also something shared. Think of Iago on Othello's besotted love for Desdemona: 'His soul is so enfetter'd to her love / That she may make, unmake, do what she list, / Even as her appetite shall play the god / With his weak function.'

Who chose these passages? Bishop or Milly? They couldn't tell you. It felt to both as if these passages had chosen themselves.

She didn't get into RADA.

Her married sister Elsie, who had just had a stillbirth in the sixth month of pregnancy, was sitting at the kitchen table – staring at a crust of toast. A crust of toast: the sounds represent the focus of her conversation, from the loss of her baby to the loss of her baby. 'They've taken samples from the uterus. They're running tests. But they don't know why.' She sat in her raincoat and floral headscarf. Occasionally, she clicked open the gilt clasp of her handbag, took out her red purse, opened the purse and poked among her change. She was like someone woken up on a bus with only one memory that doesn't make sense. She put away her purse and sat there breathing through her mouth. Her nose was blocked. Two tears hung on the line of her chin, fell and were replaced by another two.

Milly was watching her sister carefully.

In the silence, the noise of the letter-box's ragged diminuendo.

'It's my letter from RADA,' Milly said and left the room. It lay on the doormat, a dim throb of light. She brought it triumphantly into the kitchen and laid it on the table so her mother and Elsie could see the franking. RADA – THE FIRST STAGE TO THE STAGE.

Then she tore it open with her index finger and read the unfolded letter.

'I didn't get in.' She thought. 'I shouldn't have gone for Iago.'

Elsie looked at her, took in the hurt. 'Oh, Milly, I'm so sorry. It meant so much to you, I know.'

Milly turned on her furiously. 'Who cares if you're sorry? Who cares if you care? Who gives a shit what you think? You have no idea what this fucking means. You haven't the faintest clue.'

And she left the room. They heard her run upstairs, the slam of her bedroom door.

Six months later she was offered a place at the Central School of Speech and Drama and she accepted.

The End of the Affair

The three years Milly was at the Central School, the affair continued. Bishop was entirely of her interest – prepared to discuss teachers, techniques, career tactics indefatigably – whereas the young male undergraduate actors were always competing, despite the thespian myth of solidarity and mutual support. And the ones she found attractive were not immediately attracted to her. (Slightly to Milly's surprise. She had forgotten how plain she really was.) Valuable time would be wasted on pulling focus, getting properly lit, playing her subtext, upstaging several other attractive girls. Central School wasn't short on beauty.

Milly watched her contemporaries wasting their nights on love and that bit of the day left when they'd got out of bed. Milly was in bed by eleven and spent her evenings working or at the theatre. She was lucky. Bishop was already in place, booked in advance, always available, now his divorce with Barbara had gone through – if she wanted to be laid, he was laid on like electricity and gas. And his job meant he wasn't around the whole time. She could concentrate on herself and her acting.

They didn't live together, even after the divorce. 'I need my sleep. I need my space. If I need a fuck, I prefer the afternoon when I'm not too tired to concentrate.' It also meant Bishop would be easier to offload when the time should come. She lived at home with her mother.

After a year at Central, she was known to be the exceptional actor of her intake – men as well as women. RADA tried to poach her – offering a scholarship with nil tuition fees. Her initial impulse was to reject it rudely. But it was typical that she discussed the merits and demerits of the offer with Bishop before she turned it down. No percentage in being emotional. Probably no one at RADA remembered her unsuccessful audition.

(They did. The girl they had unaccountably preferred to Milly for the final place was brilliant at the baffled, blinking ingénue but not much else. Milly was already known for her range.)

They turned it down, she and Bishop, because Milly wanted to acquire a reputation for steadiness. She could see that the good trouper image was useful in her profession. The soldiers didn't like it if they could see promotion in your demeanour. It wasn't useful to be known as ambitious. Or ruthless. Or egotistical. Milly quickly learned to present herself to her fellow professionals as just another self-deprecating professional with a stock of funny anecdotes against herself. In conversation, she listened, laughed readily, didn't talk much, chewed the inside of her lip, shrugged, deferred. In the end, she had to have a little operation to have a cyst removed from her mouth – the result of all that modest reticence, all that self-effacing silence, as she chewed her lip, bit back her retorts.

After Central, she was quickly successful. She had good parts in West End shows and enviable notices. What was known as her 'under-age Gertrude' – 'she must have had Hamlet before she was 16' – was particularly celebrated. Slightly to her irritation: Milly felt she'd aged for the part sufficiently, without any obvious 'old' acting. She thought her acting subtle and successful. The critics couldn't forget she was straight out of Central. The knowledge stopped them seeing how *really* good she was.

They were wrong. (When aren't they?) She didn't read as anything other than right for the part – the right age and the right temperament, the temperament of a sexy, rather ugly woman, grateful to Claudius for so sincerely wanting to fuck her.

Bishop began to irritate her. At parties he was openly star-struck. Milly wanted him to be cool. At this level of success, her social manner had changed. Although she could still be self-effacing if required, she adopted a confident self-pres-entation. Without being outspoken, she spoke out – calmly, in her lovely authoritative natural mezzo. And occasionally, when she had had too much to drink, let people glimpse her ebullient arrogance. Bishop called it her 'ape'. 'Chimp-chimmery-chimp-chimmery, chimp-chimp-charee,' he'd sing. 'You let him see your inner ape. You shouldn't.' Milly was irritated by the accurate diagnosis. Bishop knew too much about her. It made her feel uncomfortable.

It wasn't that she wanted anyone else particularly. She just didn't want to be unavailable because of Bishop. The affair was never broken off. It was starved to death over a period of three years. Milly answered his long emails curtly and late. 'No time. Can't write now.' She didn't return his calls or his texts. She explained to him angrily that she was busy 'being an actress', that 'this business takes work', that 'parties were work, were part of the way you got parts', so she needed to go to them on her own.

Milly wanted Bishop to hear something in her tone – the sound of a door being silently shut, until its final gasp was faintly audible.

In the end, he heard. All told, it had taken ten years.

Desert Island Discs

At the centre of the green baize, the red light went off and the green illuminated. Milly heard the intake of breath as Pompilia Rice, the presenter, began her introduction.

'She's won a fistful of Tonys, six Baftas. She's been described as the Queen of Broadway. She has a fan club in New York. She's been described as the actors' actor. She's Mildred Warren, Milly Warren.

'Milly, all these awards, all this unanimous respect within your profession, sell-out shows in New York – and yet somehow you aren't a star. Or you're an invisible star. Milly Warren, are you ever stopped in the street?'

'I never set out to be a star. I set out to be an actress. I think to be a star you need to be beautiful. I look like old Mother Reilly now. I'm 64.' Milly's versatile face was empty. Her voice was warmly humorous.

'So, Milly, is it true, can I ask you, that Ruari McGuire wanted to have an affair with you when you were both on the set of *Sunset in Tuscany*?'

'Actually, yes, it is true. Unlikely as that may sound.'

'And he was – what? – thirty years younger than you?'

'If not more. But I broke his heart. I turned him down.'

'Not many women would turn down such a star, so handsome.'

Milly laughed again. 'Come on. He was only half serious. He was really in love with my work. I had my career to think of. I didn't want the bad publicity. Think of all the women who'd hate me.'

Her first disc was played. Milly made no attempt to communicate with the presenter. She listened to the music: Gluck's 'Che faro senza Euridice', sung by Janet Baker.

'My guest this week is the actress Milly Warren. Milly, you never married.'

'No, but I've had a full sex life. Even if it hasn't included Ruari McGuire. Anyway, I'm famously married to acting.'

———

'As I said in my introduction, you're the actors' actor. But you don't conform, do you, to the received idea of a successful actor.'

'You mean I'm not beautiful.'

'Well, shall we say you have an interesting face?'

Milly lifted her large chin. 'I was beautiful once. For quite a short period.'

———

'An English teacher who helped me see that I could be an actress. Made me read Shakespeare. Took me to see things at the theatre. I couldn't have done it without him. He saw what I had before I saw it myself. I might never have seen it.'

'So you owe him a lot?'

'Everything. But I'm afraid I wasn't very grateful. I was young and the young are ruthless.'

'Are you still in touch?'

'No. I broke his heart and destroyed my own.' Milly's level, neutral voice paused. 'Well, I didn't destroy it completely. You need it to act. But I have a bonsai heart.'

———

Her Desert Island book was Bulgakov's play *Molière*.

'Because in the play Molière forgives the disciple who betrays him to Richelieu.'

Two tears hung from her chin. Her voice was steady.

———

Bishop didn't listen. He was teaching still – at another school – now that the age of retirement had gone up to 70. Somehow he missed the repeat on the BBC iPlayer.

PART VI

All I Want is Loving You – and Music, Music, Music

Hans von Bülow

This is a photograph of Hans von Bülow towards the end of his life. It's black and white but looks sepia because of von Bülow's deep ox-blood suntan. Under his eyes are mud-packs of wrinkles, but he is obviously thriving. The straight nose. That firm mouth. The high brow that once seemed destined for baldness. There is still grey hair on his head, cut short and centre-parted. As a young man, he wore his hair long – down to his jawline – in emulation of his mentor and future father-in-law Liszt. A pageboy bob. In this late photograph, taken professionally (Studio Oldenburg, München), he sports a spread-eagled Kaiser moustache, whereas in his professional prime he favoured a moustache and goatee like a propeller.

He is wearing a three-piece salt-and-pepper lightweight tweed suit. He has a high stiff-starched collar, a fortress of steep china, shielding two flourishes of black silk. He is smiling at someone we can't see: his second wife, Marie.

In this photograph he doesn't look like a man famous for being a cuckold. He looks more like the virtuoso pianist and brilliant conductor who championed the music of Brahms, Tchaikovsky and Richard Strauss, as well as that of Wagner, who took his place in the bed of Cosima von Bülow, despite an age difference of twenty-four years.

Everyone knows the story. (It exists in another version with imperious Kafka and slavish disciple Max Brod.) Von Bülow, a talented composer himself, bows to the genius of Wagner and serves his music selflessly, conducting the premières of *Tristan und Isolde* (1865) and *Die Meistersinger von Nürnberg* (1868), although he is aware that Wagner has fathered two children, Isolde and Eva, on his wife Cosima. In other words, a high-minded *Nebbich* who is pitilessly exploited by the ruthless Wagner, who spent his life taking what he needed whenever he needed, regardless of who the rightful owners might be. Everyone knows the story.

The story is wrong.

A Conductor's Perquisites

One of the five sopranos auditioning for Agathe in *Der Freischütz* wore a pink dress flounced from the pelvis but so tight at the top you could see she was completely flat-chested. The whole of her upper torso had the hard slimness of a young boy. Von Bülow thought he could make out the flat pit of her belly button. The big, squat conical nipples were unambiguously prominent through the dress material when she took a breath. Her face was beautiful – androgynous and aware of it. You could tell from the surprisingly short swept-back dark brown hair which did nothing to minimise the firm jaw and the handsome aquiline nose.

And she could sing. She finished her audition piece and met von Bülow's appraising gaze from the piano. As he handed back her music, his eyes contained a question. Will you? At first, her eyes simply returned his look, devoid of expression. Then she let her eyes smile. He wedged his cigar in the cleft of the ash-tray.

'Would you mind lifting your arms, Fraülein Bellowski?'

Von Bülow wanted to see the sweat from her armpits darkening the pink to maroon.

'And now turning?'

She turned.

'Thank you.'

At this time, in Fraülein Bellowski's frank assessment of him, Hans von Bülow was stout, without being soft or fat. He was more like a muscular pink pig, covered with coarse hair and with hard fat over the muscle.

He had none of her slimness, hard as a folded ivory fan.

Von Bülow was about to spread her. Not immediately. In due course. In the natural order of things.

Cosima von Bülow

'It's so hurtful.' Her grey eyes welled up. She had sent
Daniela and Blandine, her two daughters, to find feathers in
the garden. She took a handkerchief out of her reticule and
blew her long nose. She sat, waiting for the water to boil,
like a woman with a bad cold. The wings of her nostrils
were pink and varnished. The wick wound like a tapeworm
in its cloudy oil, and the flame under the kettle was bent out
of true by the slight breeze from the French windows.

Wagner wasn't quite sure what to say. He hadn't expected
this intimacy, this confidence. He couldn't say that music
was full of philandering, so why the fuss? Singers wanted
work. Conductors controlled the jobs. They took their
tithe. He undid his frock coat and leaned forward, his hands
on his knees. He looked straight into her, as he might if he
were going to ask a woman to bed. The eyes were sad,
serious, sincere, intent. In his deep baritone, he said, 'Our
profession is full of temptation.'

He waited a minute before adding, 'So it's hardly surprising
that Hans should have succumbed this once. You should try
to forgive him. The male is weak.' He spread his short fingers.

'It isn't just once. Hans has been unfaithful right from the start.' She didn't know this to be true. Hans had neither confessed nor been caught in flagrante. There were nights, though, when he hadn't returned from the theatre, unable to get a carriage and sleeping in a chair (he said) in his dressing room. And she noticed too that with each new production, his sexual interest in her was at first intense, then dwindled to nothing until the opera closed. Cosima inferred arousal, then satiation.

Wagner toyed with the tassel on his velvet cap. 'Schopenhauer says the universe is driven by blind, impulsive will. *The World as Will and Idea.* He says that goodness can only exist, if this will is repressed. But it is difficult, very difficult, to control this essence, this force. It has no altruism. There is no altruism.'

He was thinking of Herwegh, who had introduced him to these pessimistic ideas of Schopenhauer. Which were also an adulterer's charter. Herwegh, the poet, who had cuckolded Herzen. Not that Herzen was a paragon of chastity. His wife was paying him back with Herwegh. Also. In addition to falling in love.

The arithmetic of adultery. Arithmetic was too complex. The barter of adultery. The barter of bodies.

Wagner wondered whether Cosima might consider a revenge fuck to hurt her husband in return. In due course. Obviously not now. Now, she was wronged by a husband she loved.

He accepted the cup of tea and lifted it to his wary lips.

My Mother and Henry James

In Chapter 4 of *What Maisie Knew*, Henry James introduces Mrs Wix, the unlikely moral centre of his novel, squinting through her 'straighteners', greasy-haired, vulgar, common. But a mother – as Maisie recognises for the first time in her short life. Mrs Wix's daughter, Clara Matilda, has been killed in a road accident: 'she [Maisie] found herself deeply absorbed in the image of the little dead Clara Matilda, who, on a crossing in the Harrow Road, had been knocked down and crushed by the cruellest of hansoms.'

There is, unmistakably, an ironic dimension to that superlative 'cruellest', which hints at a detachment comparable to that of Stephen Dedalus, who considers the death of another young girl in a hansom accident – pierced, fatally, through the breast by a sliver of glass. Stephen thinks the incident cannot be tragic, as the newspaper report described it, because it doesn't conform to his definition of tragedy, his interpretation of Aristotle's pity and terror.

The irony, in this case, is directed against the young man's callow preference for theory over experience – over common sense.

To return to Mrs Wix and her dead daughter, James strikes

his ironic note early: 'it was comfortably established between them [Maisie and Mrs Wix] that Mrs Wix's heart was broken.' It would be too easy to upbraid James for the bachelor complacency of that adverb 'comfortably'. What does Henry James know about the death of children?

In *Portrait of a Lady*, when her son Ralph Touchett dies, Lydia Touchett says to her niece Isabel Archer: 'Go and thank God you've no child.' Mrs Touchett has forgotten that Isabel knows what it is to lose a child. About three hundred pages earlier, Madame Merle tells Ned Rosier (and us), 'She had a poor little boy, who died two years ago, six months after his birth.' There are two possibilities. That Lydia Touchett has forgotten Isabel's loss and James wishes to underscore her moral coarseness. Or that Henry James himself, a childless bachelor, has forgotten Madame Merle's parenthetical disclosure. I think it is the latter.

But, while James may not know what it is like to lose a child, he is extremely acute about the peripheral manifestations surrounding the central event at the time and afterwards. He certainly captures Mrs Touchett's desire to monopolise the death, her sense that it ministers to her own importance.

Nor should we condemn him for that adverb 'comfortably'. There is a difference between the death of a child and the figure that death makes in the memory.

In 1939 my mother's first child, Norma, aged three, had

convulsions and died under my mother's hands on the kitchen table. She was pregnant at the time and miscarried with the shock. Sometimes she spoke about this and about the funeral, where she saw a rat in the cemetery.

In 1998 I took my mother to Venice with my wife. It was the first time my mother had been outside England. She was going blind but could see enough of Venice to be appreciative. We stayed at the Savoia e Jolanda on the Riva Schiavoni – in two rooms with a balcony overlooking the lagoon. On the last night my mother was a little tipsy and started to consider her tragic life, how hard things had been for her. She felt sorry for herself and started to cry.

The death of her daughter, her husband's disabling epilepsy, my brother's polio, my brother's prison sentence for demanding money with menaces and acts of gross indecency, her nerves, the hard work and sleepless nights working as a dress-maker doing alterations. These tragic particulars were dissolved. They were dwarfed by her sense of injustice. She was a tragic heroine centre stage in her own imagination – moved by what she had gone through, her spectacular suffering.

The events themselves no longer touched her by now.

The dull eyes of the child, tipping away, returning. The projectile vomit. A minute of mild shivering.

I think of that young woman at the kitchen table, her terrible fear.

And disbelief. Her knowledge that none of this is true. It has happened too quickly.

The shock in her. That young woman, recalculating, replaying the rapid events in the hope of a different outcome. Taken by terror. Beginning again.

She is too busy for sorrow. Too afraid. There are tears, but tears are beside the point.

Life is dead in your fingers. As if you have blown out a match by accident. It is dead in your fingers.

Reluctant Richard Wagner

Wagner was right to be wary.

He hadn't forgotten his flight from Zurich. What had possessed him to jeopardise his musical interest – the ample cottage on Otto Wesendonck's estate, the subsidy, the salary, the settlement of debts – by an infatuation with Mathilde, the silk merchant's wife?

We like to think there is a link between sexuality and creativity. Picasso is often cited to confirm this glib equation. But only consider the quiescent Henry James – and think again.

We think that Wagner was a satyr, a womaniser, sexually driven, priapic, a pouncer, a cynical lecher. This cannot be correct. Look at the dates. Otto Wesendonck extends his hospitality and his purse to Wagner in 1852 out of admiration for the composer's music. The affair with Mathilde Wesendonck doesn't begin till 1857.

It lasts for one year, then Wagner is asked to leave. Mathilde seems to have kept her husband informed. We can assume either that Otto Wesendonck was a complaisant cuckold, or that the relationship was intense on Wagner's side but platonic on both. The result of this relationship was the

Wesendonck Lieder and *Tristan und Isolde.* Perhaps the adjective we need is Arthurian – courtly love.

Wagner takes five years before he is completely certain that Mathilde will be receptive. Then he makes his move. He speaks his love. He doesn't lay a finger on her. He is content actually to finger the fingers of her white, pipe-clayed kid elbow gloves. Wagner is more interested in love than he is governed by lust.

(Let us not exaggerate the sexual impulse. Only in rapists is its imperative categorical.)

I have loved you five years in silence.

Irresistible.

It has been enough. I want nothing in return. Except your presence.

Wagner is forced to leave by the incontinent behaviour of Minna, his long-suffered wife. Her scenes are unacceptable. Publicity is unacceptable. Wagner leaves, alone, for Venice.

Here he is at San Zaccaria, in debt, the sun in his narrow eyes, his hair lifted at the back by the breeze, staring across at Salute. His clothes smell of sweat and eau de Cologne. Mathilde is turning to music in his head. A consummation devoutly to be wished – more than physical consummation.

His beard might be a brace for a broken neck. Under the chin he is proud of and reluctant to hide. It has some of the improbable bespoke contrivance of the gondolier's rest for his oar. You look at the Wagner beard and wonder why.

———

Wagner needed von Bülow more than he wanted the man's wife. The man could conduct. He was going to conduct *Tristan*.

So what was it?

It wasn't self-destructiveness. He was neither a gambler nor an alcoholic. All right, he *was* a gambler. Risk was exciting. But he went to the tables not because he had a passion for gambling but because he was in search of passion.

He went to women, then, in search of passion? Partly. He wanted the women to ignite something dispassionate in him that watched women appreciatively but indifferently. He would like to be compelled. In thrall. Listen to the music of *Tristan*.

But, most of all, Wagner was like a child solicited by circumstance. Here was a sharp knife. Here was a piece of new wood. You could harm the wood. So you harmed the wood. You were wooed and won by impulse. You acceded to the inertia of events, invited by circumstance.

Wagner was like wood. Rigid, dull, serviceable, solid. But in the presence of fire, according to the chemist Primo Levi, suddenly suicidal.

But there had to be fire.

And Cosima von Bülow, with her pink nostrils and lank blue-stocking hair, had little to offer beyond an unsettling resemblance to her father Franz.

She was to be the greatest love of his life.

How did that happen?

What was the fire?

Nymphenburg, München, the Villa von Bülow

It was three o'clock on a hot afternoon in Nymphenburg. The front doors of the von Bülow villa stood open. Wagner could see the larger hothouse like a heliograph in the distance through the open back door. It took his eyes a few moments after the brightness outside before he was accustomed to the darkness. A huge bee, like a date dipped in caster sugar, grappled with the edge of a cut-glass bowl filled with visiting cards. It took off, intoxicated, humming to itself, and fell to the parquet floor. Clocks gleamed and ticked loudly in the silence.

Somewhere, a distance away, a cuckoo imitated a cuckoo's hyphenated call.

Wagner mounted the broad wooden stairs to the first landing. The door of the nursery was wedged open. The two little girls, Daniela and Blandine, were asleep in their white-painted cots. Blandine's fingers were loosely bunched next to her face, and her mouth now and then made sucking motions. A fine fizz of sweat could be seen at her blonde hairline. Her eyes were not quite closed. Next to Daniela's parted lips on the pillow, a dark saliva Sardinia.

The nanny's fingers were locked under the steady rise and fall of her bosoms. Head tilted, her mouth open, she slumped in an armchair.

The family were taking their afternoon nap.

Carefully, Wagner tiptoed past the closed doors on the landing. The furthest door was open the slightest of cracks, through which he could just see, quite close, the face of Cosima von Bülow. Her oily eyelids were closed. But she wasn't sleeping peacefully like her children. She seemed to be having a troubled dream. Her breathing was shallow, slightly hurried. And then her mouth opened gradually, as if someone were hurting her, until she turned her head and jerked.

Like someone startled awake – without ever opening her eyes.

Wagner watched her closed, shining eyelids and went on watching them until they opened and were aware.

Aware of what?

Of something. Of being seen.

When she rustled down the stairs five minutes later, she found Wagner reading the *Süddeutsche Zeitung* in the drawing room. And she knew who she had been seen by.

From now on, he looked at her differently, he talked to her differently. It was subtle, but she could tell his interest was piqued. She was too quenched now, but she wanted him to know she knew. And he, of course, now needed to be that close to her again. He desired her look of ugly excitement.

So it was only a matter of time.

The date on the *Süddeutsche Zeitung* was 16 June 1864.

Force the Moment to Its Crisis

Yet they seemed, Cosima and Wagner, to find it difficult to advance their situation. Or even articulate the situation. They weren't often safely alone. The nanny behaved as if she were part of the family and would enter and walk wordlessly across the room, working her jerky haunches. The girls ran and flounced, perched on the arms of the furniture, lay whispering to themselves on the floor.

But if they had tea together, there were long silences in which they looked at each other.

Cosima was waiting for Wagner to declare himself.

But he couldn't be sure what their situation really was. He had seen her masturbate. Rather, he hadn't seen her masturbate. He had seen the orgasm on her closed face. They had made eye contact but without her darkened vision knowing with what. With whom. Neither knew what the other knew. Neither knew what the other wanted.

Weeks passed. It was July.

And, into this mystery, breezy, ebullient von Bülow, smacking his lips, rubbing his hands, burping, singing bits of *Tristan* and *Tannhaüser*, tickling his daughters, tossing them up to the ceiling, carrying them, one under each arm. Hans was in high spirits. Rehearsals were going well. The score was in his head. He had sacked two singers. He had been rude to a horn player: 'Herr Kieslowski, kindly vacate the chamber pot.' (He was fucking Isolde and he had felt up one of the chorus.)

As von Bülow was pretending to be a dragon with dyspepsia on the verge of eating Daniela and Blandine, Cosima said, under the girls' delighted screams, 'You saw me. Doing that. I want you to know I know.'

Wagner was white. He swallowed visibly.

'I want you to know that I like it. Being seen by you.'

He nodded. As if assenting to a difficult proposition.

Which, in a way, he was.

The Children

At this time, 1864, Daniela was four and Blandine just three. By April 1865 Cosima had given birth to Isolde, knowing the child to be Wagner's. How did she know for certain that the child was not von Bülow's? And if she was so certain, how was von Bülow persuaded that the child was his?

Suspicion. Human beings are not suspicious. They are naturally trusting. Except when they are in a foreign country. Abroad, unsure of the exchange rate, everyone is suspicious. But think how unlike us in our normal state this paranoid angst is.

Jane Austen says in *Northanger Abbey* that one's neighbours are voluntary spies, unpaid, but spying isn't the same as being suspicious. Paying attention to what goes on, being nosy, being curious, is one thing. Being suspicious is another. We have to pay people to be suspicious – like store detectives, customs officers, copy-editors, the IRS, actors in search of a subtext. Or novelists interrogating dates, chronology, motivation, behaviour.

Von Bülow's only reason to suspect his wife would be his own behaviour, as he worked his way through singers and chorus. Otherwise, he had no reason to suspect his wife or his friend Wagner, the composer he most admired in the world.

We *know* that Cosima was being unfaithful with Wagner. So we think von Bülow should be suspicious. But von Bülow knows nothing, suspects nothing. The guilt Cosima and Wagner feel is invisible to von Bülow – partly because they are extremely careful not to arouse his suspicion. Their behaviour is exemplary. Wagner rents an apartment in Nymphenberg – close enough and far enough away from the von Bülow villa. The apartment has a concealed entrance and can be approached down a little lane from a different street. They never arrive together. They leave separately. No hotels.

Before she is pregnant, Cosima's sex with von Bülow is intermittent – his appetites already supplied by singers – and oral, anal, manual. It is all about his sexual pleasure, Cosima now reserving hers for Wagner.

As soon as she misses her period, the sex is vaginal. 'Mmmm, we haven't done this for a bit. *Very* nice.'

No one remembers dates. Even the suspicious don't remember dates.

(They could tell him. But Wagner needs him to conduct *Tristan*.)

Tribschen, Lake Lucerne

But of course there were spies, paid spies, intelligencers in the service of Ludwig II's ministers – ministers worried by the influence of Wagner on the King. On 15 August 1865 an item appeared in the *Süddeutsche Zeitung* under the headline 'Triangle in Orchestra'. The anonymous author fulminated, in his feline way, about the 'open scandal' of Wagner's 'illicit' relationship with Cosima von Bülow, apparently sanctioned by Herr von Bülow, the conductor at the recent première of Herr Wagner's opera *Tristan und Isolde*.

'Our friend the deft skulker appears unaware of the oxymoron: how can an affair be "illicit" and "open"?' Wagner affected to be grimly amused.

'It's open now,' Cosima replied. 'For a fact.' She was anxious about her imminent confrontation with von Bülow.

'And now it *is* in the open, let it be in the open. *En plein vu.* No more lying.'

Cosima thought. 'We *haven't* lied. To anyone. We haven't had to, up till now.'

Wagner was tougher. 'You don't think Hans will think he hasn't been lied to?' He shook his head.

'Sins of omission?'

'You didn't want to hurt him.' Wagner's sentence was an instruction as well as a statement of fact. Fact in so far as it went.

'Or your music.'

'Or my music,' Wagner agreed.

They sat in silence for a time. Wagner picked up a silver coffee spoon and held it bridged between his index fingers. He was thinking, moving the spoon towards and away, as if looking for the optimum position. Calculating something. A measurement.

'It's a pity,' he said, still staring at the spoon, 'you can't tell Hans that you love us both.'

————

'I'm no angel. You know I'm no angel. But this …'

Von Bülow slid a cigar out of his shagreen case. It contained six cigars and was called the Syrinx Cigar Holder. He held the Villiger to his ear and listened to its spectral crepitations as he rolled it in his fingers. He used the cutter and moistened the tip in his mouth. The flame from the long Lucifer swayed like a lazy flag, pulled by von Bülow's breath, let go, inveigled, let go, enticed.

Until the end of his cigar was excited.

'You feel betrayed.' Wagner put his fingertips together. 'Of course. That's natural. Very natural. It's also conventional. But you have to realise that her feelings for you haven't changed.'

He paused. 'Look. You love my music. You love the music of Brahms. Do I feel betrayed?' He smiled. 'Yes, I feel betrayed. A little bit of me feels betrayed. But I am ashamed of my insecurity. You are not being unfaithful to Wagner. You are being generous to music.'

Von Bülow smoked. His eyes were full of tears, honeycombed with tears.

Wagner took the stopper out of the whisky decanter and lifted his eyebrows interrogatively. Von Bülow nodded and as he did so two large tears rolled down his nose.

'When you bed a singer – our lovely Isolde, for example – whom I envy you – do you stop loving Cosima? No. You continue loving Cosima. Otherwise you wouldn't feel betrayed by her. You wouldn't care.'

Von Bülow raised his big hand in protest. 'Brahms was better. Better analogy. Cosima isn't having a side-dish of Wagner. You aren't a talented tenor with a tremendous tool that everyone's heard about.'

'It isn't about sex,' Wagner said. 'It's about love.'

'And that's why I feel afraid,' von Bülow said. 'That she loves you more than me.'

'As you love Wagner more than Brahms?' Wagner couldn't resist.

'Yes.'

'Neither of us is dead. Each of us could write something which would eclipse the other in your admiration. In your love.' Wagner lifted his whisky in a kind of toast. 'Hans, nothing stands still. Not even love. Love changes all the time also. You know that. We both know that. We have to face that truth. It is part of love's greatness. Her love for you has changed, as it will change again, and again. But still she loves you. That hasn't changed. Talk to her. You'll see.'

———

But when they talked, the von Bülows, another, breathless worry had surfaced.

'Is she mine? Is Isolde mine?'

'Does it matter? Yes, I can see it matters. All right. All right.' Cosima made calming gestures with both her hands. 'I could lie. I could say I was sure she was yours. I'm 80 per cent sure, 90 per cent. Let's not go into the details.'

'Yes. Let's go into the details.'

'Why? They won't convince you if you're unconvinced in advance. You'll only be pained. You could be the father. You're more likely to be the father. Just take my word for it.'

'I can't. The details.'

'No.'

'Why not? What are the details that make it more likely that …'

'That you are the father, not Richard? They're *his* sexual details, Hans. I wouldn't tell Wagner what *you* do in bed.'

'Come on, Cosima. Don't you see how painful it is, not knowing? It can't be more painful if I know.'

'You're asking me to betray Richard.'

'You've betrayed me. He's betrayed me.'

She shook her head and reached for his hand. She squeezed it. 'Only if you choose to be betrayed.'

After a moment, she made her decision.

'Mostly he prefers to masturbate.' She paused. 'Every combination. Is that enough detail? Because if it isn't …'

It was true in so far as, had she been compelled to choose, it would have been her own sexual preference. Otherwise, it wasn't true.

It was a strategic lie, a tender lie, and a lie that von Bülow found perversely exciting, even as it pressed on the deep bruise of betrayal.

She also liked being pinned and penetrated.

In fact, the *Gesamtkunstwerk* of sex.

Had she told von Bülow these facts of life, he would have suffered a haematoma of the heart. She didn't want to hurt him. That wasn't a lie. But she would hurt him if she had to, hurt him to save her happiness.

Bavarian society, represented by the *Süddeutsche Zeitung*, was outraged by the reconciliation between the parties, the equanimity displayed. Neither Wagner nor the von Bülows condescended to respond in public or in private. They were gods. It was beneath them, this scandal. They dripped disdain and indifference. They were calm.

Here is Wagner polishing the nap of his top hat on his sleeve, smiling at the king, and visibly unwounded. A window of brightness.

Here is von Bülow with his ready smile, offering a Monte Cristo cigar to a pretty mezzo, who laughs and shakes her head. A chorus of laughter from the chorus. His sexual confidence is strangely undented.

Here is Cosima like a Renaissance madonna, half smiling, with a bright nimbus of nonchalance. The steps of the carriage receive her feet, stoop under her descending feet. She affects not to notice these underlings, but is careful never to stumble.

So it is only a matter of time – again – before the King is forced to ask the composer to leave München. Ludwig offers Wagner the use of the Villa Tribschen on Lake Lucerne – where he can finish composing *Die Meistersinger von Nürnburg*. Whose première will be conducted by von Bülow in June of 1868. Cosima accompanies Wagner to Tribschen in December 1865, leaving von Bülow behind, but taking her three children.

The principals seem reconciled, irritatingly untroubled. Except that von Bülow has an episode of ill-health – facial palsy and slight paresis in his conducting arm. Technically, a motor-sensory deficit in his right arm and a contralateral facial deficit, suggestive of a brain infarction.

Infarction is what medics call tissue death caused by loss of blood supply. In other words, von Bülow was missing his children.

He recovered in time to rehearse and cast and conduct *Die Meistersinger* in June 1868. In October he granted Wagner and Cosima the divorce they now desired.

A Footnote about Ann Golding

I loved her very much. Shortly after William Golding died, my wife and I went to visit his widow Ann at Tullimaar, their Cornish house in Roseland. By then she was quite old. Her skin was shrivelled chiffon and she was wearing chiffon as she settled herself on the sofa with some difficulty. She was made up. Gay. Tough. 'I haven't cried,' she said, half triumphantly, half plaintively. She had a slight speech impediment.

'No, you had a stroke instead,' my wife said.

She was like a dead baby wearing lipstick, puffy, wrinkled, floating in formaldehyde.

PART VII

Find the Lady

Princeton

They met for the first time in Princeton. Both of them visitors from England. Two heterosexuals about to have a lesbian affair – the first for each of them.

Prospect magazine had sent Steph to interview Paul Muldoon, Howard G. B. Clark '21 University Professor in the Humanities, Professor of Creative Writing in the Peter B. Lewis Center for the Arts, Poetry Editor of the *New Yorker* and a likely prospect for the Nobel Prize in Literature.

'What is it about his hair?' Steph asked.

'You get used to it,' Assia said.

'It's coastal, don't you think? Meant to be casual, Bob Dylan Afro. But it's like a whin bush on a cliff top. Off Portnoo or Carrick. Or some other dump in fucking wind-tormented Ireland. I remember going for a walk in one of those places. Got an amazing headache in seconds from the wind parting my fucking hair in a hundred different places. Every which way. I thought I had a brain tumour. Seriously.'

Steph talked like her father. Cliff the Riff, performer, journalist, professional piss-taker by appointment. Rude, take-no-prisoners, go with the lava flow, toss it off before there's time for second thoughts. Thank you and good night.

Assia Horwell laughed. She was 34, a visiting F. Gus Danielli funded 'professor' from Bristol, teaching Rhetoric 6139 for a semester. Her department in Bristol had a reciprocal relationship with Princeton. Her Princeton replacement was teaching one of her modules, either 'Modernism and University Modernism' or 'Realisms in the Novel'. She couldn't remember which. Whiteladies seemed a long time ago. Since she was a Canadian citizen, Assia immediately fitted in at Princeton. She was comfortable there in a way she wasn't in her adopted country.

Just the same, if not quite comfortable, quite successful.

She was the current Susan Sontag figure in the UK literary scene – without the skunk hair; she was blonde – pulchritude and profundity. Unbeatable combo. Every time. TV loved her. She lived in London and did the commute to Temple Meads twice a week. She was divorced, with an eight-year-old daughter, Tamsin Hardy. Hardy still taught classics at Saskatchewan. Assia preferred it that way. He could remember what she was like before she was Assia Horwell ('Good *eve*ning') with the steady, low voice and the bright smile and the confident stream of intelligent but uncontroversial opinions. When she was Peggy.

Steph was 42, unmarried, undivorced, and looked as if she were 28. Her father had forbidden her to smoke or drink.

'Fucks up the skin. Look at me. Foreskin face.' He puckered his mouth like a prepuce and did his cough. He had two versions. His bronchitic wheeze with phlegm obbligato that went on for over a minute and required fantastic breath control. Or the demented double Alsatian bark with choke-lead conclusion. Today it was the acoustic bark. He made her learn two languages in her gap year. Italian and German. 'Don't want you living on your wit like me. It's fucking hard to be funny when you're frightened. Only a few of us can get away with it.' She had just ended a three-year relationship with a barrister who was writing a novel because he was bored by the bar. Steph knew he'd never make it as a novelist. He had a theory of jokes, but he'd stopped making her laugh – even on the page, where the jokes could be planned, set up and detonated with 'military precision'.

'How did that fucking phrase – "military precision" – ever gain any fucking credence? It's been fucking axiomatic since the first fucking stone was thrown that military operations are always a fuck-up from the second watches are synchronised.'

Steph wasn't sure whose riff this was, whether it was hers or her father's.

It was hers. But by now she wasn't to know that.

She was small, dark, cropped, sexy, serious in repose, with a sudden smile that surprised her whole face. The Holy Grail of grins. A beauty spot on her left cheek shone like patent leather.

The waitress gave them their menus, recited the specials ('as if they were special needs'), returned to take their orders, set their food in front of them. They ate, decided against dessert, paid and left.

They liked each other.

'Maybe see you in London?'

'Sure.'

They liked each other, but didn't think to exchange telephone numbers. It had been fine, warm, fun, but nothing special. A minute after saying goodbye, they were each thinking of other things – confirming flights, phone calls, packing, presents, shopping, class, paper grading, a review to write.

First Kiss

They met again at the Cape summer party in Bedford Square under one of the great plane trees. It was almost a year later. The party was in full swing. There were lanterns in the trees.

'Hey.'

'*Hey.*'

'How are you? Let me introduce you to my dad. This is Cliff. Dad, this is Assia Horwell. We met up in Princeton. When I was writing that profile of Muldoon.'

'The one with the stuff about arseholes, I mean hairstyles. From Lyle Lovett to Paul Muldoon: Arseholes with Hairstyles. That the one?'

'Fuck off, Dad.'

'You didn't read this piece?' Cliff asked Assia.

'Dad, she was in Princeton.'

'Someone in Princeton might have brought it to her notice. Muldoon, for example. Paul Muldoon with the Pompadour.'

'Dad thought I shouldn't have mentioned his fucking hair. It was one fucking sentence.'

'One fucking *long* sentence. Look, I have to dash.' He held out his hand to Assia. 'Deadline. Nice to meet you.'

They watched him work his way towards the gate – evading greetings and plaudits, gliding like a skater, slipping sideways through the crowd with speed and grace, unstoppable, untouched, unimpeded. Cliff had given up drinking on his fiftieth birthday. He was 60 now – and he still smoked.

'Arseholes with Hairstyles. That wasn't the title of the piece, by the way. And I never mentioned Lyle Lovett. That's him. Just doesn't like it when anyone else tries to be funny. He knows he's funnier, you know. Trouble is, he's fucking right.'

It turned out that Assia was writing a book for Cape. Steph and Cliff were just good furniture. And still sharp when everyone around was losing theirs.

'So what's your book about?'

'*Chicks with Dicks: Multiple Sexual Identities.* Exploring the inner Other.' It came out pat.

Steph's grin arrived. 'Arseholes with Hairstyles.'

Assia grinned back. 'It's less loony than the title sounds. A bit less loony.'

'So was my piece about Muldoon. So it's theory, right?

Have you ever actually fucked another woman?'

'No.'

'Have you ever wanted to fuck another woman?'

'No.'

'Have you ever, in any circumstances, or at any time, kissed another woman with sexual or erotic intent?'

'Nope.'

'Neither have I. Come here. I think we should give it a try. No big deal. OK? Tongues OK?' Steph was being her father. Licensed.

They kissed.

'You know, wine tastes really funny if you don't drink. I mean sour.'

'Isn't sour sexy?' Assia replied.

'Sometimes. I know what you mean. What you're thinking about.' And Steph's grin arrived again. 'How was it for you anyway?' Steph asked.

'No big deal.'

'Oh, I thought it was nicer than that. Just a bit sour.'

This time they exchanged mobile numbers.

They made 'Londoner's Diary' in the *Evening Standard*. The quotes: 'No big deal' from Steph; 'We were researching my book' from Assia. The headline: BEDWARD SQUARE. *Private Eye* picked up the story and did one of their fusions so it was Peter Mandelson snogging Gordon Brown. Caption: 'Licking the Lords into Shape'.

How the Thought of You Lingers

Steph and Assia evolved a protocol. If they met in a public place, a restaurant, a café, the Tate Modern, they kissed, not on the mouth, but on the cheek – three times, *à la Russe*. A tiny tango of touch. A ritual they ironised by mwaahing noisily.

In private, they avoided all physical contact.

————

'Would you like to stay the night?' Assia was a little drunk.

'I can drive. I haven't been drinking, remember.' Steph raised an eyebrow.

'I know you haven't. I meant would you like to stay the night?'

'Stay the night in italics, you mean. Or fucking inverted commas. Right. Gotcha. What about Tamsin?'

Steph was surprised it was so matter-of-fact.

'That's not a worry. She's nine, for God's sake. Course she might always join us. She sometimes comes for a cuddle in the middle of the night.'

'Are you sure you want to try this, Assia?'

'Why not? It was that kiss. I think about it. Don't you?'

'Sometimes.'

'It crosses your mind?'

'Sì. In the distance. I give it a wave. I say hi.'

―――――

They undressed in the dark, whispering.

'There's a toothbrush in the cabinet. I mean a new tooth-brush head, a spare. It pisses me off the way they make you buy two.'

'Where do they fucking get off, eh? Is there any floss, Assia? I have to floss or I can't get to sleep.'

'On the side of the basin. Why exactly are we whispering?'

Assia could hear Steph's smile in her voice. 'Whispering. What a fucking relief. I thought I'd just suffered a massive hearing loss.' She was doing her deaf voice with its loud auto-incomplete: 'heary lore.'

They lay under the duvet, totally still, still not touching, smelling of peppermint and peppermint and Pinot Grigio.

'I didn't realise lesbianism was going to be so torrid. Or that the inner Other would be worried about having the window open a crack. Can we have the window open a crack or I won't get to sleep?'

'Kiss me.'

'Assia, I think this is a *terrible* idea. What if I want to fart?'

'Fart.'

There was a silence.

'Whose nose is whistling? Is it me? Or is it you?'

There was no answer.

'Assia, please, can we have a fucking window open? Then we can go to sleep and forget all this stupid ... You're not pissed off with me, are you? You don't think I'm a cock tease? Or a twat tease, I suppose it must be, mustn't it?'

'Steph?'

'What?'

'Shut up and go to sleep.'

But in the morning Steph was sitting on Assia's face being rimmed when Tamsin came silently in through the bedroom door.

'Where's Mummy?'

Steph opened her eyes. Tamsin was staring sleepily at her tits and scratching an elbow. Now she was being slowly sucked.

And then the sucking stopped.

'I think she must be in the bathroom.'

'I've been bitten by something. An insect or something. Itchy.'

As Tamsin turned away, Steph saw her bum had bitten off a bit more nightie than it could chew.

The door closed with a click and both women were out of bed.

'*Christ.* Steph, there's another dressing gown in the chest of drawers. Bottom drawer.' She was arranging silk paisley around herself – one, two – and tying a brisk bow.

Our brilliant, our virtuosic motor skills, how reliable they are. How rarely we are paralysed with fear.

Though that's exactly what it felt like to Steph less than a minute before. *The Loved One.*

The Male Gaze

Steph liked the way Assia's thighs spread as she sat on the toilet. Resting her rubber dinghy. Rounded. The red marks left on her legs by her elbows. The imprint of the seat on her seat.

She thought lesbians liked women who looked like men. But she didn't like Assia because she looked like a man. Which is what she half expected. She liked Assia because she looked like a woman. As if she, Steph, were a man. Looking at Assia the way men look at women.

It was the redistribution of weight according to gravity that held her gaze. It was the way she was water seeking its level, finding the only solution. Always the soft option. It was engineering and magic accommodation, this female metamorphosis. Gravitational give and take.

She liked the hang and weight of Assia's breasts. She liked the way they moved when she walked without her clothes. Describing a pattern she couldn't describe. A series of simple movements she couldn't quite grasp.

Simple but somehow contradictory. As a drop of water fattens, stretches, shrinks: undecided in the suspense of its own elastic eternity.

Or Find the Lady.

She liked the way they slewed sideways when Assia lay on her back. The way they shone in the shower. She liked the size of her flat nipples. The way Assia's nipples differed from her own. They gathered and knit. Her own were smaller, harder.

The way Assia's arse hung, broad, to its slope just below the top of the thigh, continuing out below the buttocks.

From waist to pelvis to tapering ankles: a coffin-lid lozenge. Her big sprinter's buttocks.

When she drew up her knees and presented her buttocks, the arsehole's café au lait. Its spicy *Lebkuchen* taste. Her rank ragged furrow. Its exciting ugliness.

The two dints at the base of her back above her behind. What did they mean? They seemed enigmatic, strange, profound to Steph.

It was the fusion of delicacy and sturdy strength she found herself falling in love with. Steph surprised herself.

And she surprised Assia. Who wasn't so sure.

Strike the Father Dead

For Assia, homosexuality was an experiment – interesting, enjoyable enough, but an experiment. In advance, she found the element of perversity exciting – until it no longer seemed perverse and felt routine. The truth is, Assia wasn't naturally passionate or particularly sexual. She looked the part – apparently perfect casting for the sex goddess – but it was only acting. Not passion but a pastiche of passion. She knew what she was supposed to do. She hit her marks. She was quick to take cues. She was well trained in theory but ungifted in practice.

As they do, a protocol evolved in bed: Assia should always come first and always be the first to come.

Steph needed nothing except Assia's naked presence to be solid, sore-throated with excitement, almost painful to touch. Her orgasms could wait in the stack before landing in sequence with a shudder, a jerk, a shake and sometimes an ooze of smoothness. Whereas Assia's faint fire had to be coaxed and kindled, subtly tended and fed before its brief blaze.

Steph was the trembling temple slave, kissing the icons in their filthy corners, getting smacked for her trouble. She was literally the underling. But Assia had no real interest in being the dominatrix. She felt miscast and envious of Steph. She might prefer to be degraded, subservient herself. How could she tell? Steph had taken the part. 'Smack me. Smack me. I'm dirty.'

And the sex reached out into their larger relationship. Initially, Assia had been attracted by Steph's no-nonsense manner, the way she could cut through the crap with a No. 2 iron, her fearlessness. Now and then she still glimpsed it. In a Sicilian hotel, the Villa Igiea outside Palermo, Assia saw Steph drag a local taxi driver by his lapels from his cab to the front desk. He was attempting to overcharge them. Steph established the proper fare and contemptuously counted off a salad of notes from the fan of Euros in front of her.

But mostly what Assia saw now was fear. Fear and dependence. Fear of Assia's laconic kiss, her sexual torpor, the sense of an ending. It wasn't attractive. It wasn't amusing.

It wasn't sexy.

So it wasn't Assia's fault, the way she felt.

———

In the end, Steph decided to consult and confide in her father.

He knew already. They sat together, watching Assia on

Newsnight Review with Mark Kermode, Bidisha and Armando Iannucci.

'Of course I fucking know. Everyone knows. The reason you don't know everyone knows is 'cos it isn't fucking news any more. No one talks about it. There used to be a troupe of dancers called Hot Gossip. Not fucking Permafrost Gossip. That's why you aren't in *Heat* – that and the fact no one's really heard of you. Or her. Christ, this is piss-poor, isn't it? She's supposed to be the heavyweight, right? And Kermode, he's the driver on the Clapham Omnibus. Well, he looks the part, Clapham common, with that tsunami quiff on him. Your bird *looks* OK, but she's George Steiner-lite.'

'George Steiner is George Steiner-lite, Dad,' Steph observed dispassionately.

'Fuck *off*. Listen.'

Assia was talking about Banksy. Her ensemble – her golden hair, her easy grin, her health, her brain – were working out without breaking sweat. Going through her routine routines. You could say Banksy was an outsider, an iconoclast, on the one hand. You could equally say Banksy was complicit with the consumerism he satirised: his art was, like Warhol's, dependent on the syntax of commercial art. His aesthetic was fundamentally comfortable, though his message was indignant.

'I get it,' Cliff said. 'She's got the fucking fence right up her arse because she's always facing both ways.'

They watched another item before Cliff switched off the TV. 'She should be wearing fucking leg-warmers, mascara and a mohair muffler five yards long. I should be her manager, her Max fucking Clifford Clifford. It's all about the look, isn't it? What she says is university kapok. What's she really like?'

That was what Steph wanted to know. She only knew what Assia was like – and that had changed. Except of course on television.

If Cliff knew about their relationship, he didn't know the detail. And Steph didn't supply it. 'See, Dad, she doesn't say that much any more. It's all work. Seminars to prepare for, you know. Conferences. Articles. Reports. You know when you tie a bit of dental floss around a skin-tag?'

'It gets sore. It goes black. It falls off.'

'I'm going black.' Her eyes filled. 'She says nothing's changed. But she's brushing me off. I can feel it. Everything she says. Everything she does. Testing the tag. Picking. Tightening.'

'Steph, she isn't worth it.'

'I know, but I can't help it. Thing is, I love her. And the fucking withdrawals are killing me. I have to have her now. Oh fuck. I stepped into a trap. It was my own fault. My own fucking mistake.'

None of which, when it came to it, stopped Cliff from fucking Assia.

Fucking Assia

'Men are much much more fucking primitive than women, if you think about it. The male genitals are frankly fucking crude by comparison. Take temperature regulation, for example: the scrotum ascends or descends a few fucking inches. What a feature, huh? The penis is almost as budget. A piece of pipe with a dual fucking function. Urination and impregnation. Impregnation is impossible unless the penis is stiff. Urination is impossible if the penis is stiff. Just in case you get fucking confused – a fucking safety catch. If you took the argument from design seriously and you considered the penis, you might conclude that the God of revealed fucking religion is a bit of a carpenter if not exactly a cretin.

'But then you turn to women. Wow. If you compare the genitals to mobile phone technology, the penis is like one of those early mobile phones the size of a fucking brick. It hasn't advanced beyond this blunt efficiency. Whereas women have always had Intel Inside. The clitoris is the fucking microchip. Women have always had iPods and BlackBerrys. Fingertip access to a multitude of fucking functions.'

Women liked it when Cliff delivered this riff on genitalia.

Other than Steph, who was family and a testing ground for material, it was reserved for sex. Sometimes he used it to seduce them. The aphrodisiac of laughter. Sometimes he flattered them with it afterwards.

Which was the case now. Assia's head was thrown back, laughing delightedly. It was the case that women liked it when Cliff delivered his CL-IT riff.

Cliff liked it less when, a month later, purged of expletives, Assia delivered it on national TV as if it were her own – a contribution to Channel 4's new fifteen-minute *By Women, For Women: Aggressive Essays*.

'I fucking saw you on the fucking Slit Slot, you thieving little cunt,' Cliff yelled into his Ericsson.

'Oh, come on, Cliff,' Assia honeyed. 'Intertextuality. Nothing is new. Read Barthes.'

'And you've got no, repeat *no*, comic timing.'

How did this come about? That a 62-year-old man should be fucking the lesbian lay of his heterosexual heartbroken daughter?

It was the crudity of his equipment.

And his small man's lifelong weakness for big women. Not fat women. Big women on the same scale as big men – but totally female, hyper-female. What he called the Über-wench. (He was very fond of women's athletics on television. But not the distance events. He would be sad when the playing career of Serena Williams was over.) Cliff hadn't realised the size that Assia came in. TV was deceptive. He wasn't smitten because she was smart. And he couldn't work out why she hadn't made more of an impression in Bedford Square.

But it wasn't that Cliff fucked Assia, though he may have thought so. It was that Assia fucked him, or let him fuck her. She was in charge.

She fucked him for three reasons.

He was funny. She wanted to know if he was funny in person for periods of over ten minutes. (The length of time they'd talked at the Cape summer party.)

They met because Steph wanted to know where things stood. She thought that Assia might be more frank with her father. (She was. She was. She opened up all right.) Assia agreed to meet 'off the record': she was curious to meet 'Keith Allen with a college education'. (Or, a more complicated slow burn, 'Damien Hirst without a degree from Goldsmiths'.)

Then something odd happened. He reminded her of Steph when they first met – of all the things that had made her attractive. The wild humour. The lack of restraint and calculation. The lovely recklessness. (Steph took after her father, so Cliff was bound to resemble his daughter.)

And Assia wanted to end her affair with Steph decisively. Sleeping with Cliff meant there was no going back to being lesbian. It was, thought Assia, a conclusive way of sending a message.

Except that Cliff wouldn't let her deliver it.

'Are you crazy? You can't *do* that. You can't. I fucking love her. Don't you dare fucking tell her that.'

'What? That her father is fucking me now and feeling guilty. But still feeling me up.'

'It just isn't necessary for us to fuck her over so we can. Can fuck, I mean. Finish it with her without saying that.'

'Cruel to be kind.'

'I'll kill you if you do. A fucking promise, that is.'

Assia smiled. 'Don't be so melodramatic, Clifford.'

'And don't fucking call me Clifford. I hate it.'

His conversation with Steph wasn't easy. He hated lying. So he told her the edited truth. His cock in Assia's fanny, like a bit in a drill, airbrushed out of the picture.

'Steph, she wants it to end. I could say that she's sorry and upset – make it easier – but she isn't. She only pretends to be. She's fed up. Irritable. Impatient. What she says is the usual fluent set of contradictions. But she's bored. And she's frightened of being bored. Being settled with someone means being bored. She'd like to spend her life at a fucking cocktail party, looking over your shoulder to see who's next.'

(He could sense his time with Assia was limited.)

'You seem very expert on Assia for only one meeting.'

'I'm making it up as we speak. I mean, you sit there, listening and not really thinking. It's only afterwards, you know, it comes to you what the whole thing really meant. Under the fucking words.'

'Didn't you like her at all?'

'Yea, well, I can see what you see in her. It's just that I can see a little more than you see in her as well. There's something ruthless there. And something slightly terrified.'

'Can you be "*slightly* terrified"? Of what?'

'Of being found out.'

'Aren't we all afraid of being found out?'

To Cliff the question seemed alive with static.

'I don't mean of what we might have done. I mean terrified of what might not be there. A real person.'

'Dad, I can't believe I'm hearing this twaddle from you. It'll be existential angst next.'

'That's more Assia's bag, wouldn't you say? What I mean, Steph, is that there isn't enough there to break your heart over. She's an egotist, but she's insecure. And she's right to be insecure. She isn't *that* fucking bright. Where would she be without lip-gloss? In somewhere like Saskatoon.'

'You know her ex still teaches at Saskatchewan? You winkled out a lot in a couple of hours.'

'Lucky dip. I didn't know. To the point. She's less bright than you are – by a long fucking way. And she's bored by you. So she's got to be stupid. Too stupid, nothing like interesting enough for you to be broken-hearted over.'

'It isn't her mind, Dad. Her personality. It's her body. Can you believe it? I can hardly believe it myself.'

He could believe it.

———

There was no need for Cliff to detonate Assia's destructive message to Steph, as it happened.

She managed to send it anyway. When Steph watched Assia ripping off her father's riff on Channel 4, she worked it out. Two days later she hanged herself from the kitchen doorknob. Her email account was emptied. She left no note. What she left was a new screensaver on her Mac, which showed her sudden smile like a conjuring trick.

PART VIII

Without Acknowledgement

In Flagrante

He caught them in bed together, his wife and her lover.

He had suspected nothing.

Something had been bothering him all morning, a vestigial anxiety he finally located in his left wrist. He had forgotten to put on his watch, a slim gold Omega hardly the thickness of a communion wafer. But there was no abreaction even though he had located the site of the trauma. His wrist felt neurotic, anxious, strangely guilty. The lightweight watch increased its pressure as the morning moved timelessly and therefore slowly on.

What was wrong with using his mobile to find out the time? It wasn't a watch.

Angus was one of those men who consult their wrists whenever they mention any unit of time, shooting their cuffs at all twelve months, most centuries, the seasons … 'It was a week, maybe ten days' – and there he was, turning his wrist.

So he decided to drive back home and pick up the watch from the oak chest of drawers in the bedroom, where it lay in the sun next to a jar full of loose change. Slim Danaë –

naked, spread, golden – stretched out, sunbathing, and waiting for the shower of coins. Angus narrowed his eyes: yes, sunshine thickened, became palpable, a currency of light.

He let himself into the flat quietly, glanced into the empty drawing room – nothing moved, the books on the shelves observed a minute's silence, a *Vogue* lay on the green glass table-top like a *corpus delicti*. Then he ran silently up the stairs to the little landing.

(His mother – dead now – used to say he'd be the death of her, giving her all these shocks: it was like having a cat burglar in the house. Angus was rather proud of his movements, their muteness, their swiftness, this sense of silent film. He felt he could fall from any height, land without a noise and strut away like a super-model down a runway.)

As he opened the bedroom door – the porcelain surprisingly warm in his hand – he saw his watch and he saw the lovers in bed.

They were asleep.

Half turned away from each other.

Angus closed the door quietly, twinkled down the stairs, opened the door and drove, watchless, the twenty miles back to work, his heart big in his chest and noisy as a night club clubbing.

He spent the afternoon at his desk, unable to work because he was unable to think. Not because he was thinking about the consequences of what he had seen. He could only think of what he had seen. The two heads. His wife's half-open mouth.

Once, Angus had gone to his doctor with a pain in his lower gut. Quite severe. He hadn't been able to shit for a week. Laxatives, supplied by the chemist, hadn't worked – a 'softener plus a shifter', liquid paraffin and senna. He was asked to lower his trousers and the doctor felt his gut with the palm of his hand – pressing with the palm of the other. 'Does that hurt? Does *that* hurt? What *kind* of a pain?'

'Is it anything serious?'

'It could be. It could be a blockage and a blockage in the gut is always serious. Come back in a week if you haven't had a BM by then. (A motion.) If you haven't, we'll know it's serious.'

You walk out into the sunlight – except it was raining quite hard, shattering on the pavement – and your life may have changed completely. Be about to end, in fact. But there you are, feeling for the catch of your umbrella, watching water pour down the piece of wizened black elastic that hangs from the rim, as your feet get wetter and the bottoms of your trousers darken.

All you can do is wait.

Angus didn't realise how long he was prepared to wait. Or

quite why he was prepared to wait. But he didn't want it to end. Not now. Or not quite now.

Not that this stopped him fingering the pain.

At supper, he said, 'I came back to the flat earlier. Forgot something.'

Janice was gently tossing a salad – mozzarella di bufala, pomodorino tomatoes, basil, with roasted morsels of saddle of rabbit – and said, without looking up, 'Sorry I missed you. I went to the library. Ran into Brilliana.'

'That is one fucker of a name, isn't it?' Angus said. 'What were her parents thinking?'

'Wouldn't be so bad if she didn't so clearly believe in what's it called? Nominal destiny.'

'Nominative determinism.'

(Was it because he'd gone back for his watch that Angus felt that this affair was all about time? Time the healer. Time the destroyer. Isn't it about time we … Just passing the time.)

'Do you ever see Conrad Porter around the place?'

'I think he's dropped me,' she answered, 'since I said I couldn't write a paper for his seminar group. He's like that. All smiles when he wants something. Completely ruthless if he doesn't get what he wants. What do you think of this rabbity thing?'

And so they made conversation. Passed the time.

I Want a Divorce

Angus worked as a solicitor, specialising in divorce, for quite a large firm located in the small village of Farringdon, twenty miles from Oxford. Bodell, Wentworth and Mercer calculated that the reduction in rent, the larger premises, the rural environment, compensated adequately for the commute. (Oscar Bodell also happened to have a large country house a mile outside Farringdon in six acres of parkland surrounded by classic Inglesby iron fencing.)

Ten years had passed since that revealing moment in the bedroom. Nothing comparable had occurred. Angus had taken care it never would. He seldom arrived unannounced. He stuck to an established routine. 'I hate surprises.' He remembered a children's party where the conjuror had plucked a squirming, pink-eyed albino rabbit from a very large top hat, screwed immovably to the floor-length baize tablecloth. Its back paws lashed out powerfully and left raised red score marks on the back of the conjuror's hand as he warded the thing off.

When he listened to clients and pushed the box of tissues towards them, he sometimes wondered why they went through all this pain – disclosure, recriminations, financial loss – when they could simply avoid it. Step aside. Let it pass.

'Not even a hotel. He had her in *our* bed. There was a condom under the pillow. Used.'

The tissue box made a sniff, sniff, as Angus moved it across the desk like a man placing a bet in a casino.

'The most disgusting pictures. Women in gas masks being burned with cigarettes.'

'He just said that whores didn't mind doing that stuff. The enemas.'

Not all of his business was sexual. Now and again, a couple would decide they were incompatible because one was bent on a retirement bungalow in some bleak seaside town in north Wales, when the other wanted to be in Bath, 'near the grandchildren'.

Sometimes it was sexual only in the sense of being non-sexual. 'We never had sex. Not even at the beginning. He never laid so much as a finger on me. Actually, I didn't mind, you know. Then Roger came along.'

There was a widespread madness here that people talked about only in Angus's office.

When he looked back to that morning ten years ago, it was equally a mystery. Why did he simply turn away? Partly out of politeness. As you would if someone had forgotten to lock the lavatory door. And they were asleep. It had the semiology of innocence. A row would have meant waking them. He was devastated by the discovery, but he had looked away, his body had decided to leave before he could think. He didn't know. Even now.

But he felt that if he had made his bed, he should lie in it. The cliché provoked a stiff smile like a stale sandwich.

Janice and he went together to see the Mike Nichols film *Closer*, with Julia Roberts, Clive Owen, Natalie Portman and Jude Law. Four jealous people talking nakedly.

'He tastes like you, only sweeter.'

'You should try eating pussy.' 'I have.'

'Thank you. Thank you. Now fuck off and die, slag.'

Angus couldn't help feeling the film was unrealistic: shockingly realistic, unsparing, filthy-mouthed and minded – but unrealistic. This wasn't the way that people behave. Not even in Angus's office with the Kleenex to hand. Disclosure was the price you paid for divorce. The film was a version of how people would like to behave – would like to have behaved – if they were braver, more passionate, more outspoken, more heroic. More like a film. The psychology was wrong. As stylised as *Brief Encounter*, actually.

The more likely scenario. A wife sitting at the kitchen table pushing a tip of love letters towards her partner, saying only, 'I want a divorce.'

Or: 'I read your email account. I'd like a divorce.'

Angus had never trusted Janice since that day. Certainties

vanished. Or were likely to vanish without much surprise. It was like the Blitz, when Bolsover Street became impassable overnight. Or when a redesigned traffic system creates a one-way nightmare. You could live through a war. You could live with a longer drive to the station.

It was no longer ideal.

If it was torture, it was sleep deprivation – mild enough but regular, nightly – and you could live with it.

But it's tiring being betrayed.

The Sexual Imagination is Transgressive

Why couldn't he say 'I want a divorce'?

Because he found it difficult to say anything. Even in his sleep, his reticence was unsleeping.

Because, when he saw the two of them, sleeping there under the duvet, the force of betrayal made him realise how much he loved her. He didn't feel murderous. He felt depleted. He felt bereaved. As if he had lost her forever in that moment.

Sudden death. *Sudden death.* Taking a few seconds. As if the person had disappeared. And couldn't be found.

But he could have her back.

Angus discovered too that his heart wasn't broken, exactly. It wasn't torn either. It was bent. Love still worked, but it worked differently. His sexual imagination was drawn to ideas of infidelity, enriched by ideas of infidelity.

In the end, he wanted to speak to her out of this rich seam of excitement. But he couldn't bring himself to speak. Her breath was shortening, then lengthening, then shortening, as she took another run at her orgasm. A series of no-jumps.

He wanted her to suck six men at once. Force down their tight foreskins and let them squirt on her fanny.

He wondered if perhaps he wasn't slightly homosexual.

(He was. A bit. Aren't we all? A little bit?)

Her climax leaped with a grunt of effort.

What was she thinking about?

She was thinking: I would like to push your stiff red aaah into another woman's aaah. And she came.

One night, as she turned her struggling face away, she managed to say: 'I like thinking about fannies.' But his hearing was getting worse. He couldn't hear and she wouldn't repeat it.

She had a fantasy about women in short summer dresses sitting cross-legged so you could see all of their upper thighs – but their privates protected by a point of dress. The lap of the dress. Different knickers behind it. Some fannies with full Brazilians.

Infidelity was something they used. Without acknowledgement.

You wouldn't have thought it to look at him. The weekday solicitor in his two business suits – the pin-stripe and the chalk-stripe – consulting his watch. Or, relaxed at the weekend, in cashmere cardigans, Viyella shirts, baggy red socks. His greying hair allowed a bit of licence for a couple of days.

And always angst – wondering if innovations in their love-making originated elsewhere.

The Royal Festival Hall

It was the great cycle of Mahler symphonies. They arrived an hour early, parked on Waterloo Bridge and bought a couple of toasted sandwiches. Angus needed a piss, left Janice reading the programme at their table, and went looking for a lavatory, following the signs till he found a gents in a faraway corner down a dark corridor.

The man next to him was masturbating quite openly, shielded by a slab of porcelain. As he turned to leave, Angus glanced in his direction and saw the erect penis. He didn't bother to wash his hands, but hurried out into the dim corridor. He took three or four steps, then returned to the urinals, took out his stiff penis and showed it quickly to the man.

The man, bearded, bald, nodded in the direction of the stalls. There was a streamer of wet toilet paper on the tiled floor. A freckled toilet bowl.

It didn't take long. The man had a piercing in his prepuce which he adjusted to release his wet glans. He undid Angus's zip and took out his penis, weighing it in his hand, then knelt to suck it. Fifteen seconds.

'Now you.' These were the only words spoken during their

encounter. He pulled down Angus's head and came in his mouth. It was intensely sour. Angus gagged, spat and turned away, so the rest of the semen shot into his ear.

The man buttoned his fly and left. Angus waited a few seconds, then went to the washbasins and cleaned his ear and hair with his handkerchief.

As he walked towards Janice, who was waving as if he were lost, he felt light-headed, as if he had smoked a cigarette.

During the concert, he reached to feel his hair with his hand, where it had stiffened like hair lacquer.

He knew he never wanted to do that again.

Yet found himself wishing, during *Das Lied von der Erde*, that their penises had managed to touch. Head to head.

————

'Sorry we're running so late. Unexpected emergency early on. What can I do for you, Angus? Statins OK?'

Dr Mulholland was a fellow Rotarian.

'I'd like an AIDS test.'

'OK. Any particular reason? Anything you'd like to talk about?'

'No. Precautionary. I don't in fact think I'm HIV…'

'But you'd like to be on the safe side. Fair enough. I'll make you an appointment with the nurse. She'll take your bloods. Would you like to know the result by post? Or would you prefer to drop by the surgery in a couple of weeks?'

'I can drop in when I'm passing.'

'Go to reception. They'll fix a time with the nurse.'

———

As he looked at the printout with the test results – negative, negative – Angus thought for the first time that Janice could have given him AIDS.

Could have. But he knew that she hadn't. Just knew that AIDS was unlikely.

She Knew He Knew

She knew he knew. Had always known.

How did she know he knew?

Because they both heard him open the Chubb on the front door – the thing they most feared and never forgot to listen for.

There was hardly time to whisper.

'Janice. Fuck. Fuck. What do we do?'

'Sleep. Pretend to be asleep.'

So Janice lay there, listening, listening, eyes closed, mouth a little open, feeling her heart rate. Listening. The slight vibrations from his feet. The faint scrape of the door on the carpet. The fainter scrape of his breath from bounding upstairs.

Then silence. Was anyone breathing?

More silence. Surprising silence.

Faint vibrations from his weight on the stairs. Listening. For the second sound of the Chubb. Like a word in a foreign language. Its secret, unintelligible consonants. *There.*

A minute, or less, in which everything had changed.

When Angus had gone, Janice opened her eyes and looked at the ceiling. Then she swung her legs out of bed and stood trembling, unsteady as an invalid. A small black rubber dildo fell out of her body on to the grey carpet, almost silently.

'Brilliana, you've got to go. But give it ten minutes, just to be sure.'

And the two women embraced, their hearts awkward, massive, in their chests. Neither of them had anything useful to say.

They dressed, made the bed, sat in silence on the edge of the counterpane – Russians before a journey – then Janice looked at her watch and nodded. Her mouth was dry when they kissed and her breath smelled. She felt as if she were running a temperature.

Mrs Kipling's Heartbreak

In 1892, when he was the most famous writer on the planet, Rudyard Kipling contracted a severe pneumonia virus in New York. It was front-page news. The King and the Kaiser sent him telegrams of well-wishing. More importantly, perhaps, Kipling's six-year-old daughter Josephine fell victim to the same virus and died.

Kipling's wife, Carrie, returned from her daughter's burial to be at the bedside of Rud. His condition was so critical, he wasn't told that Josephine had died. As she was entering the sickroom, Carrie realised she was wearing only black and she snatched up a red shawl, draping it across her shoulders.

I wonder what it is like to know your daughter is dead and that her death is a deadly secret, possibly fatal. That you have eaten from the Tree of Knowledge in all its inedible bitterness and are forbidden to spit it out. You are forced to swallow and smile.

Kipling had three children: Josephine, John and Elsie (the youngest and only survivor). John was killed at the Battle of Loos but reported missing. He was only 19. He had poor eyesight, like his father, but Kipling lied and pulled strings to have his only son accepted by the Scots Guards. At the celebrations for Armistice, Kipling wrote to another bereaved father, Sir Hugh Clifford, on 18 November 1918: 'Glad you escaped the peace celebrations. I bolted home from town and had my dark hour alone.'

Critics who arraign Kipling for sacrificing his son don't seem to understand that Kipling didn't want his son to die. John Kipling dies for Kipling's principles and stupid patriotism. He isn't a son, in their account, he is a cowardly proxy, a pitiful pawn.

I am sure Kipling would rather have died himself. This obvious truth, this obvious human truth, escapes many humanists hostile to Kipling's values. But all you need is charity – the charity to credit Kipling with a father's feelings.

This is his poem 'My Boy Jack', 1914–18:

> 'Have you news of my boy Jack?'
>   *Not this tide.*
> 'When d'you think that he'll come back?'
>   *Not with this wind blowing, and this tide.*
>
> 'Has any one else had word of him?'
>   *Not this tide.*
> *For what is sunk will hardly swim,*
>   *Not with this wind blowing, and this tide.*

'Oh, dear, what comfort can I find?'
  None this tide,
  Nor any tide,
Except he did not shame his kind –
  Not even with that wind blowing, and that tide.

Then hold your head up all the more,
  This tide,
  And every tide;
Because he was the son you bore,
  And gave to that wind blowing and that tide!

PART IX

Work Experience

Olly

Olly was tall, 18 years old, hardly ever combed his hair and worked in editorial as a temporary assistant to Frank Pierson. He was going to Oxford the following autumn to read English at Christ Church. He wrote witty, incisive reports on the fiction he was asked to read. And he was quick – reading and writing. It took him half an hour, sometimes slightly less, to draft a decent blurb.

'Will you email Brian Shelley and ask him who we should send proofs to for advance praise when the fuckers come in from the printers? He must have some friends still. Christ, though, there's nothing worse than one of those half-hearted endorsements, is there? But ask, they arrive, and you have to use them.' Frank popped another lozenge of Nicorette and continued combing his hair over a blank piece of paper.

'"Brian Shelley has done it again." "Brian Shelley pursues the goal of all writers – he is trying to turn the world into words." "*Horizontal Haze* fumes and shimmies in its quest for authentic Africa."' Olly was enjoying himself. 'But the good ones don't work either, do they? You know, "Fucking masterpiece, Leo Tolstoy" – followed in short order by the inevitable "I beg to differ" from Tom Robinson, pawky, independent, in our own *Independent*.'

'Christ, he's a cunt.' Frank paused. 'Robinson. Not Tolstoy. Actually, they're both cunts.'

Olly raised an eyebrow at the piece of paper.

'Fucking dandruff. The beginning of the fucking twenty-first century and still no cure for cancer or dandruff. AIDS, big tick, Job Done, but dandruff still dancing out the range of heavyweight science. At least I've still got hair to have dandruff in.' He made to crumple the paper.

Olly laughed. 'Nah, I'll flog it in the pub. Wrap of Charlie, mate?' He slid his discreet hand convincingly across the desk.

You'd hardly know he was straight out of Winchester, had read all of Henry James (his favourite author) and could scan English as well as Latin poetry.

In his Oxford entrance interview, he was asked by the English tutor which poetry he liked. 'Ezra Pound.'

'Can you recite the first line of "The River Merchant's Wife – A Letter"?'

'"While my hair was still cut straight across my forehead".'

'Pretty good. But it's "*When* my hair was still cut straight across my forehead".'

'I really don't want to be cheeky, but I really think it's "while". Can we check?'

It was 'while'.

'OK. Very good, actually,' the tutor said. 'Can you scan it?'

'That's trickier,' Olly smiled. 'It seems completely arhythmical, doesn't it? Straight as the girl's fringe. But actually it's almost regular trochees, don't you think? *While. Hair. Still. Straight. Cross. Fore.* All take a stress.' He stuck out his thumb, his index finger, his middle finger, marking the stresses. 'I doubt if Pound said "forrid" rather than "forehead" – and "forehead" is close to a spondee. So is "still cut" in "still cut straight". That's why it's trochaic but seems arhythmical. Sorry, am I making any sense at all?'

This time the tutor smiled. 'Perfect sense. What about after that? The rest of the poem.'

'Pretty well arhythmical, I'd say. But I'd need the text in front of me.'

Then they discussed Pound's attitude to Browning, then Browning. The tutor asked about the form of Browning's 'My Last Duchess'.

'You don't mean, is it a dramatic monologue? Obviously you don't mean that.' He thought. Narrowing his eyes for five seconds or so. He was seeing the lines. 'Oh, you mean it's in couplets. I never noticed that before.'

'Clever chap, Browning. Technically much better than people say he is.' The tutor smiled: the interview was turning into a conversation.

215

'Henry James, for instance.' Olly was thinking of James's piece about the burial of Browning in Westminster Abbey. As he explained.

When he closed the door behind him, the tutor wrote on his pad: 'fucking clever', adding 'and seems very nice'.

He was both. Afterwards, he said to his teachers at Winchester he'd been lucky to be asked about his favourite poem. 'How jammy is that?'

––––––––

There was a girl in the secretarial pool he had his eye on. A little redhead, who looked half Chinese, maybe a quarter Chinese. One day, by the photocopier, he asked her out for a drink 'at the cavernous, inhospitable dump across the road with the inedible food'.

'Thank you,' she said. 'But I don't drink. I don't like alcohol.'

He smiled his smoker's smile. 'Well,' he said, 'none of us *likes* it. You could have a soft drink.'

She had a glass of water. 'Tap is OK.' He got a little bit drunk. She was, he thought, incredibly beautiful. He recited 'The River Merchant's Wife – A Letter'. She couldn't make out the words but she saw his eyes fill with tears and she sensed the shake in his voice.

'It's these wooden floors. I can't really hear. The acoustic is difficult for me.' She opened her handbag and pushed a piece of paper towards him. 'Write me the name of the poem. I'll read it in peace and quiet. I have to go home.' She got to her feet.

'So, where do you live? Maybe we're going in the same direction.'

'With my parents in Holland Park.'

'Posh. I'm heading off to West Hampstead.'

'And put the poet's name. Otherwise I won't be able to find it.'

Outside, he gestured lavishly and quoted, '"It was a warm evening, heavy with the reek of petrol." Evelyn Waugh. Brilliant. Summer in the city. Says it all.'

———

She found the poem on the shelves in her parents' drawing room and read it in her bedroom, where she couldn't be seen. It was like a love letter in a foreign language. She was afraid of poetry, so it took her some time before she worked out the situation – an arranged marriage at a very young age, 14, that had turned to love within a year. And a year after that the husband had gone on a journey. The 16-year-old wife is missing him very much. And her way of saying how much she loves him is to say she will come out to meet him as far as Cho-fu-Sa. That was like *To the Lighthouse* – one of her A-level texts – when

Mrs Ramsay says Mr Ramsay was right about the weather. Which is her way of saying she loves him. Irony: when you say something innocuous and it means the King is dead. Irony: saying the opposite of what you mean.

She was moved by the passion: 'I desired my dust to be mingled with yours / Forever and forever, and forever.' To love beyond death. To feel this and only be able to say: 'If you are coming down through the narrows of the river Kiang / Please let me know beforehand, / And I will come out to meet you, / As far as Cho-fu-Sa.' She could feel the love behind the lines.

And there was an ache in her face like sinusitis. She wouldn't be without it. It answered a need.

———

Two months later they were at Hampton Court together, watching the Thames like a flag in the wind. He was in love with her. He had given up smoking so he could kiss her. But he hadn't yet kissed her.

He turned and took her shoulders in his hands.

'Annie, I love you.'

She shook her beautiful head. 'Look at the water,' she said. 'Look at the minnows and pinheads. They're there if you look long enough. You become accustomed.'

He looked where she was pointing. Then nodded. He could see.

'You see, Olly, I have Down's Syndrome. I can pass. But I have Down's. You didn't spot it, did you? But I'm infertile. The back of my head is just a little flatter than normal. My parents – my mother mainly – managed a miracle. And I'm a little bit slow. I did A-levels, so I'm high-grade, but things are never easy. Reading isn't easy. I'm happy filing and photocopying. And you're brilliant – you are, you are – and you're going to Oxford.' She put her hand to his lips to stop him saying anything.

His lips.

'So I can't love you, Olly. I can't.'

I desired my dust to be mingled with yours
Forever and forever, and forever.

PART X

Coda

You came in a dream. Your usual difficult self. I couldn't decide what I wanted most – to kiss you, or look at you.

Who is speaking?

Anyone who is still in love with someone who is dead.

Carmen Frazer, Frazer Reid, Kipling, best beloved, Ann Golding, the man in the brown mackintosh, me.

Venezia, 26 August 2009

Acknowledgements

Donna Poppy copy-edited this novel with her legendary diligence and saved me from many factual errors, inconsistencies and solecisms of expression. She is, as many grateful authors will testify, nonpareil in her expertise. Any mistakes that remain in the text are not her fault but the result of my incorrigible persistence in error.